# Across *the* Puddingstone Dam

*For Brigid O'Neill*

# Contents

# Across *the* Puddingstone Dam

*The* CHARLOTTE *Years*
By Melissa Wiley
Illustrated by Dan Andreasen

———

# Across *the* Puddingstone Dam

Melissa Wiley

Illustrations by Dan Andreasen

HarperCollins*Publishers*

*J*

*c.1*

*The author wishes to thank Dr. Nancy Seasholes
for sharing her extensive knowledge of the history of the
Boston–Roxbury Mill Dam. Thanks also to Theresa Peterson,
Tara Weikum, and Alix Reid.*

HarperCollins®, 🏠®, Little House®, and The Charlotte Years™
are trademarks of HarperCollins Publishers Inc.

Across the Puddingstone Dam
Text copyright © 2004 by HarperCollins Publishers Inc.
Illustrations copyright © 2004 by Dan Andreasen

Library of Congress Cataloging-in-Publication Data
Wiley, Melissa.
    Across the Puddingstone Dam / Melissa Wiley ; illustrations by Dan
Andreasen.— 1st ed.
        p.   cm.
    Summary: Her eleventh year brings many changes in the life of
Charlotte Tucker and her family, including the building of a dam near
their home in Roxbury, Massachusetts, attending school, meeting her
mother's older brother, and the birth of her own baby brother.
    ISBN 0-06-027021-7 — ISBN 0-06-440740-3 (pbk.)
    1. Tucker, Charlotte—Juvenile fiction. [1. Tucker, Charlotte—Fiction.
2. Wilder, Laura Ingalls, 1867–1957—Family—Fiction. 3. Family life—
Massachusetts—Roxbury (Boston)—Fiction. 4. Roxbury (Boston,
Mass.)—History—19th century—Fiction.] I. Andreasen, Dan, ill.
II. Title.
PZ7.W64814Ac 2004                                        2003012469
[Fic]—dc22                                                        CIP
                                                                          AC

1   2   3   4   5   6   7   8   9   10
❖
First Edition

# *The Mill Dam*

Charlotte turned eleven in the spring of 1820. For her birthday, Mama and Papa gave her the new book by Sir Walter Scott, the famous novelist who was spoken of so highly in all the papers. Last winter Mama had read his novel *Waverley* to the family, holding them all entranced—from Lewis, who was nearly a man now, right on down to Mary, who would be seven in June. Charlotte especially had been captivated by Mr. Scott's tale of life in faraway Scotland, where Mama and Papa had grown up. She had been sorry to see the book end. Now there was the new one, satisfyingly heavy in her hand, beckoning with adventure. *Ivanhoe*. It was a name full of mystery and promise. Charlotte was tempted to run off and read it all alone, in some quiet sun-dappled nook beneath the blossoming apple trees. She knew, though, that the rest of the family was as eager to hear the story as she was. Tom was eyeing the book with the same expression he wore whenever Mama placed a platter of roast goose on the table. So Charlotte handed it back to Mama and asked if she would read it to the family after she finished *Robinson Crusoe*, which they were halfway through.

Besides, quiet nooks for reading were in short supply this spring. There was scarcely a corner within a mile of Charlotte's house that was free from the constant bang and bellow of construction. Men were building a dam across the Roxbury Flats. Two dams, really. The main one, the Mill Dam, was to stretch from the end of Beacon Street in Boston westward across the Charles River to Brookline. A

smaller dam, the Cross Dam, would extend
from the end of Tide Mill Lane and cut across
the flats to intersect the Mill Dam at its
halfway point. For over a year the wagons had
been rumbling past the Tucker house toward
the construction site. The tidal marsh that
had once rung with the cries of heron and gull
now lay chastened under the thunder of ham-
mers and the shouts of men.

Tide Mill Lane was not a lane anymore. It
was a road: a stern road, all business, impa-
tient with amblers and children. Mary had
nearly been run down by a team of horses last
week, and the driver had not stopped to apol-
ogize but had actually cursed at her as she
darted in terror out of his way. Papa had
walked out to the Cross Dam to speak with
the foreman. The foreman had been sorry; he
had little girls of his own at home. But he
could not, he shrugged, be responsible for the
behavior of every teamster who hauled a load
of stone from the quarry.

"I'd keep my little ones off the road, if I
were you, Tucker," he had cautioned. "Your

house is in a devil of a spot for accidents, ain't it? I don't know how you can stand it."

Mama's eyes had blazed when Papa recounted the story at supper that evening.

"How we can stand it?" she said in disgust. "What choice have we? Weren't consulted, were we, when the fools in Boston were fighting each other for a share in these blasted dams?"

"Easy, me love," said Papa lightly, in the same gentle tone he used to calm a rearing horse. "There was naught we could do aboot it then, and there's little noow."

Mama's withering glare showed exactly what she thought of the horse-calming voice.

"Dinna you gentle me, Lew Tucker," she said. "I've a right to be angry, and you ken it well." She glared across the length of the table at him, while the children looked on in silence. Papa held her gaze, his face solemn, until suddenly Mama laughed and shook her head.

"What am I sayin'? You're angrier than I am," she said. She passed a hand over her eyes. "Mary," she said, the edge gone from her voice, "stay off the road from now on, lass. All o' you. Be careful. Times have changed on Tide Mill Lane. I fear 'twill get worse before it gets better."

It was not like Mama to be pessimistic. Charlotte stared at her, troubled, but the merry light came back to Mama's eyes and she teased Tom about coming to the table with soot on his nose. Mama was unhappy about the Mill Dam, but she was not going to let it spoil a nice supper.

Nor would Mama let the dam ruin a beautiful spring. The week after Charlotte's birthday Mama sorted through the packets of seeds she had saved from last year's crop of pumpkins, squash, corn, and beans. She set Charlotte and Lydia to work planting the vegetable garden while she and Mary sowed fennel, basil, thyme, and dill in the herb garden beside the house. The two gardens were separated by a low stone wall that Papa had made long ago. Mama's herbs were famous in Roxbury—or rather, Mama was famous for her skill at brewing them into healing teas and ointments. People came from all over town to buy her remedies for gout, stomachache, and cough.

Charlotte, laboring over a long row of onion sets, wished Mama could brew a remedy for aching muscles—at least one that she would allow Charlotte to take. Mama's pain-relieving willow-bark potion was much in demand, but she never gave it to children unless they were feverish. Charlotte didn't even ask. But she and Lydia entertained themselves by thinking up tonics they'd like to invent to make planting time easier. Charlotte wanted an infusion that would make her so strong, she could lift the hoe as if it were a feather. Lydia wanted one to keep the blackflies away.

"And the mosquitoes, too, while I'm at it," she added. "They'll be along soon enough, I expect."

Lydia was fifteen now, tall and slender, her fair hair pulled back in a long tail to keep it out of her face as she bent over the rows. Charlotte's brown curls were more troublesome; the soft fragrant breeze from the flats teased wisps of hair loose from bonnet and bindings, until she thought the tickling would drive her mad. Every day when she came in from the field, she had streaks of dirt across her cheeks from brushing recalcitrant locks aside. She worked with her back to the road as often as possible, so the wagon drivers and passing workmen wouldn't see her grimy face. When Tom and Lewis came home from Papa's shop for the noon meal each day, they teased the girls for being as dirty as blacksmiths.

Whenever Tom was out of school, he spent his days working with Papa and Lewis in the smithy. Lewis, eighteen years old, was an apprentice no longer. He was a full-fledged smith now, with a smith's broad shoulders and muscled arms. He worked alongside Will Payson, who had been Papa's striker since Charlotte was a little girl.

Will and his wife, Lucy, lived down the way and across the main road at the foot of Great Hill, near the quarry. They had two children: three-and-a-half-year-old William and a tousle-headed little girl named Anna who would be a year old in June. They ate Saturday dinner with the Tuckers every week. Sometimes, on weekday afternoons, Lucy brought the children over for a visit. Charlotte and Mary kept William out of mischief—it was a two-person job—and Lydia took charge of little Anna. Lucy brought her mending, and they all sat together in the pleasant, breezy back parlor that had once been Will and Lucy's own room.

In one corner of the back parlor was an enormous widemouthed basket filled to heaping with wool, recently sheared from Mama's merino ewes. The girls had spent the first half of May helping Mama clean it: the least pleasant task of spring. Once it was clean, it must be carded. Charlotte did not mind carding as much, though it was tedious and hard on the arms.

She liked to pull off soft puffs of the wool with her fingers, and shape and twist them into little figures for Mary and William to play with. Sheep were easiest to form, of course, and tiny swaddled babies. But William preferred bears (not too difficult to shape) and dogs (which looked very like small bears, only with longer tufts for the ears). He put in frequent requests for horses, but Charlotte could not produce one that met his satisfaction—nor hers, for that matter. A horse's legs were too slender to fashion from wisps of wool.

The back parlor had a door leading directly outside. Mama liked to leave it open on fine afternoons for the wind to carry in the scent of the lilac bush that bloomed in purple abandon beside the barn, where the sheep and the milk cows lived. The rumble of wagons was not as loud here in the back of the house.

On one such afternoon, Mama was just pouring Lucy a cup of tea when Tom burst into the room, his hands and shirt streaked with smithy dust.

"Have you heard?" he panted. Charlotte looked up from her carding paddles with interest but not alarm. Papa's shop was a gathering place for townsmen with news. It was hardly an uncommon occurrence for Tom to thunder into the house with a fresh piece of intelligence.

"Someone broke into the church last night," he said, filching a gingersnap off the plate Mama had set on the little three-legged table beside Lucy. "Made an awful mess, whoever it was. Knifed the cushions in the pulpit, and—" He hesitated, swallowing his bite of cookie before delivering the worst of the news. "He—they—I don't know how many there were—they tore up the parish Bible. Pulled it to pieces."

Charlotte and Lydia gasped in chorus. Mama looked as if she might throw the teapot across the room.

"Lord have mercy," Lucy murmured. "Who would do such a thing?"

"Can we go see?" demanded Mary.

"Hush," said Mama. "What are folks sayin', Tom? Have they no idea at all who it was?"

"No, ma'am. Dr. Porter says it must have been the fruit of drunkenness, but Papa says it sounds more like spite to him."

"I wonder," said Mama. "Och—mind the baby!"

Anna, who was still wearing the long, trailing frocks of a babe-in-arms, was scooting out the door, her white skirts bunched around her knees. She heard Lydia coming to catch her and tried to quicken her pace. Her legs got tangled in her frock. Lydia snatched her up and carried her back to her mother.

"Oh, look at you," scolded Lucy, taking Anna from Lydia. "Another frock half ruined. I don't know what I'll do when she starts walking."

Mama laughed. "At least then she willna grind in the dirt wi' her knees." She sighed. "I declare, Lucy, I worry more over your bairns than I did over me own. 'Twas quieter here when mine were wee. Anna's so very quick—she could get into the road before you missed her. These miserable wagons . . ." She turned back to Tom, shaking her head. "And now this! Vandals in the church. Roxbury's not the sleepy place it once was."

"But we'll be able to walk to Boston in half

the time, when the dams are finished," said Lydia. "I shall like to go to the shops there."

"They sell the same things as Bacon's General Store," Mama pointed out. "And at worse prices, more often than not."

"All the same," said Lydia, "I can't wait till the road opens."

"I can," said Charlotte emphatically. There was so much traffic already, with the road only half finished, petering out in the middle of the marsh. She liked the idea of a shortcut to Boston—her whole life she had longed to go there, and truth be told, she thought it was plumb silly that she had not yet been—but she wished the shortcut did not have to begin at her own front door.

# *Goose and Gander*

Papa's land stretched far beyond the house toward an outcrop of Roxbury puddingstone, a kind of stone useful for building.

Puddingstone was a funny-looking kind of rock, Charlotte had always thought—dull gray slabs studded with little round pebbles, red, yellow, and brown. It looked just like its name. The bright pebbles were like raisins and nuts in a thick gray pudding. There was so much puddingstone in the area that Roxbury had been named for it—Rocksbury—more than two hundred years ago.

Papa's stone ledges had a fine view of the Roxbury Flats, but Charlotte had seldom played there even as a small child. There were more appealing places to play closer to home. Even as she grew older, she found little reason to scramble up the slanting faces of rock, so full of sharp edges and treacherous spurs. She had preferred to play in the flats at Gravelly Point, where the ocean surged into the river at high tide. There, before the workmen came, the gulls had cried their mournful songs, and ducks with glimmering green heads paddled proudly beside their drab mates. Cranes had stalked the shallows, alert for the plashing of frogs.

The puddingstone ledges were of no practical use to Papa, and when, two years ago, representatives of the Boston–Roxbury Mill Dam Corporation had sought leave to quarry stone at the site, Papa had consented. The Mill Dam was going to be built, no matter what. The city of Boston had issued a thirty-thousand-dollar bond for the purpose. Papa's nearest neighbor, Mr. Samuel Waitt, had already come to an agreement with the corporation regarding his gristmill, which was powered by a tidal creek that flowed out of the flats. Papa, like many in Roxbury, thought it better to work with the corporation (and the city of Boston) than against.

For two summers running, men had worked at the ledges, breaking out masses of puddingstone for the dam. The quarrying had progressed more slowly than expected. Old Seneca Harrington, who was hired to carry provisions to the workers at the ledge each day, reported that "workers" was hardly the name for them. The quarrymen were lazy drunkards, he maintained.

"About all them fellers have done is dig themselves out a little shelter to lie in," he told Mama, trundling past the Tucker house in his empty wagon one afternoon in June. "It's hot as blazes up there on the rocks, 'less you can get out of the sun."

Charlotte felt sorry for the quarry workers, lazy drunkards or not. June felt like August this year. It was the hottest summer anyone could remember.

"They can take their time, as far as I'm concerned," Mama told Seneca. "I'm in no hurry for those dams to go up. Roxbury'll find itself downwind o' a cesspool when this job is finished, you mark my words. The flats'll be naught but festerin' mud and rottin' fish."

Old Seneca nodded, frowning beneath his grizzled brows.

"Aye, what's good for the gander"—he jerked his head toward Boston, across the flats— "might not turn out to be so grand for the goose. Gee hah, Brown Mary!" He shook his reins, and his patient old horse trundled on down the road. Old Seneca's rusty chuckle trailed after him; he always laughed when he said the name of his mare. She was brown indeed, and he thought it a fine joke.

"What did he mean?" Charlotte asked Mama. "About the goose and the gander?"

"Roxbury's the goose," Mama explained. "And Boston's the gander. We'll not ken exactly what this dam will mean for Roxbury until 'tis built. And then 'twill be too late."

She dabbed her forehead with a corner of her apron.

"Come, lass. Let's go inside. We mustna be standin' out in this heat for too long."

Mama especially felt the heat, because she was expecting a baby. She had not told Charlotte so—it was not proper to speak of such things—but Charlotte had eyes, and she guessed.

What would it be, a brother or a sister? A brother, she hoped. There were two boys and three girls in the family already; another brother would even it up nicely. Charlotte liked things to be neat. She liked chores that were about setting things to rights or putting things together in tidy ways, like sewing and sweeping and polishing. She disliked the tasks that left a bigger mess than when she started, like making soap and cooking.

Babies certainly left messes in their wake; Charlotte knew that from experience. But they were messes easily forgiven. The Tucker house was always merriest when Anna and

William were visiting. Often Charlotte wished Lucy and Will had not moved to their own house. Anna was bound to take her first steps one day soon, and Charlotte greatly feared she would miss them.

She followed Mama through the cool, shady lean-to into the kitchen, where the fierce afternoon sun beat through the back windows. The sand on the floor glittered in the shafts of light; it was hot under her bare feet.

"Mercy," said Mama wearily. "'Tis hot as a brick oven in here."

She flicked the sheer white muslin curtains across the panes, but still the sun seemed to glare through.

"I feel like a maple candy left in the sun," said Mama. "The lads must be roastin' alive. Lottie, run down cellar and fill a jug wi' cider. You may take it over to the shop wi' Mary—if you can find her. Mary!"

Mary came running from the back parlor. Mary, who was about to turn seven, never walked anywhere. Her long red-blond hair fell in tangled waves over her shoulders; she could not keep a hair ribbon in place to save her life. Upon hearing she was to accompany Charlotte to the smithy, she cheered. Mary loved the clamor of Papa's shop.

She ran ahead of Charlotte alongside the road, taking care to keep well to the side. The heavy cider jug was cool in Charlotte's arms, a welcome contrast to the hot, dry dust beneath her feet. Clouds of dust swirled up from Mary's feet and hung in the air, heavy and dull, after she passed. It coated Charlotte's own feet with a brown film, and she knew her white petticoat would have a dirty brown stripe at the hem when she took it off that evening.

"Ugh," she said. "I wish it would rain."

"Me too!" called Mary over her shoulder. She gasped and whirled around. "Charlotte! Is it my fault? I sang the 'Rain, rain, go away' song on Saturday, and it hasn't rained since."

Charlotte laughed. "It hadn't rained the whole week *before* Saturday," she pointed out.

"Whew," sighed Mary. "That's a mercy."

A man was walking down the road toward them. He had something that looked like a bundle of long poles stuck under his arm, and with his other hand he carried a large satchel. Nonetheless he managed to touch his hat as he passed Charlotte and Mary, nodding pleasantly. He had a kind, handsome face, and his clothes, though rumpled and worn, were well made. Charlotte turned to watch him pass, wondering what the poles were. They must have something to do with the Cross Dam, she guessed, for there was nothing else at that end of Tide Mill Lane, except, of course, for her own house, and he could not be going there.

To her embarrassment, the man suddenly stopped and turned, catching her watching him. He grinned at her in a way that set her at ease. Whoever he was, he was not a drunken quarryman.

"I beg your pardon," he said lightly, "but can you tell me if I'm headin' the right way for Gravelly Point?" His R's were broad, like Papa's and Mama's.

Mary answered first, pointing eagerly.

"Aye! You just keep going until you pass a house—that's our house—and then go some more, until you come to the end of the road. When you come to a lot of men making an infernal noise by the water, that's Gravelly Point."

"Mary!" scolded Charlotte. Her cheeks grew hot.

The man laughed. "I see you're not an admirer o' the dam project, young lady," he said to Mary. "I suppose the construction is quite an inconvenience to your family?"

Charlotte could not think what to say. It *was* an inconvenience, but she did not want to be rude. Mary, untroubled by courtesy, leaped in with more candid remarks.

"My father says 'twill be good for trade, but my mother thinks 'twill make the flats smell bad and drive Mr. Samuel Waitt out of business."

"Ah," said the man, his eyes twinkling, "and who is Mr. Samuel Waitt?"

"Why, he's the miller, of course!" cried Mary, in a tone of incredulous scorn.

"Mary, hush," murmured Charlotte. "I beg your pardon," she said to the man. "Don't mind my sister. She's very young."

"I'm not! I'll be seven next week!"

"Next week!" echoed the man. "In that case, I must wish ye many happy returns."

The cider jug was growing heavier by the minute. "Come, Mary," said Charlotte. "We must get to the shop."

She said a polite good-bye to the man, and he ducked his head in another of his friendly nods. Then he turned and strode away down the road, the poles casting a long, spindly shadow on the road behind him.

# Miss Eaton's Notice

The smithy was noisy with its usual late-afternoon crowd of men. Papa was glad for the cider, and Tom and Lewis were gladder. Their heads were dark with sweat, and their faces dripped. The forge was cooling, but the air inside the stout-walled building was still heavy and searingly hot.

Papa sent the girls home with a newspaper for Mama. She liked to have one of them read it aloud while she made supper. Supper was a light meal, usually involving leftovers, so she did not need much help from Charlotte or Lydia with the preparations. But she liked company while she bustled.

This evening it was Charlotte's turn to read. The front-page news was usually terribly dull. The inside and back pages, however, could always be counted on to provide much of interest. Charlotte's eye was drawn first to the drawings of a pair of small ships floating beside the words:

## FOR SALE

*The brig ALERT, three years old, high deck, 160 tons burden. Apply as above.*

*The brig JOSEPH, 212 tons burden— 3 years old, sails fast, and well found in every respect.—For terms, apply to ADAMS & AMORY, No. 38, India wharf.*

And in the next column a wide, windswept banner proclaimed:

## JAMES BREWER
### Market Street

*Has recently received 20 pieces elegant Blue Cloths . . . Also complete assortment fine Blue Cassimeres, Satinets, Bombazens, &c. at the most reduced prices.*

There were advertisements for Spanish lemons, Virginia tobacco, and Bengal indigo. There were goose feathers, whale oil, razors, molasses, rum, and copper. Charlotte had never been to Boston's wharves, but she could picture them: the long plank structures stretching boldly over the water, lined with tall-masted merchant ships. Mama and Papa had sailed from Scotland on ships like that.

Her eye lit upon a passage announcing a new map:

25

# Map of Massachusetts,

*FROM ACTUAL SURVEY*

"Here, Mama, listen to this," she said.

*The public are respectfully informed that JOHN G. HALES, Topographical and Civil Engineer, is now engaged in making Surveys for a New Map of the Commonwealth of Massachusetts, on which will be accurately delineated the Turnpike and Public Roads, all the Rivers, Streams, Lakes, Ponds, Estates, Harbors, Towns, Villages, Churches and places of public worship, Mills and Manufactories, Mountains and Hills (with their summit heights), Country Seats, and Farm Houses, also the quality of the Sod, describing the Marshes, Meadows, Woodlands, &c. with every important object that can be noted on a liberal Scale, upon which it will be constructed.*

"What's a surveyor?" Charlotte asked.

Mama opened a jar of pickled beets. "A man who measures distances, and marks land boundaries, and makes maps," she explained. "He uses a sort of spyglass set on a stand made of three long poles. I've seen them sometimes, standing by the side of the road taking measurements of a field."

"Oh!" cried Charlotte. "We've seen one too! Haven't we, Mary!"

"Do you mean the man in the road?" Mary asked. "He didn't know much. He didn't even know where Gravelly Point was!"

"He's probably not from around here," Charlotte said. "But he had those long poles, remember? Perhaps it was Mr. Hales himself! Do you think it might have been, Mama?"

Mama considered. "Well, it stands to reason this Mr. Hales will want the new dams to be on his map. But it isna likely he does every bit o' the footwork himself. I daresay he has a team o' men canvassing the state for this survey business." She snorted. "Your gentleman will survey himself a pretty mess, he will, if he was aye headed for Gravelly Point."

Lydia came into the kitchen, lugging a pair of brimming milk pails. Her hair was twisted into a loose knot, which wobbled at the back of her head, a swoop of hair puffing out beneath it. She had just begun to put up her hair and wasn't very good at it yet.

She set the pails on the sand-strewn floor and flopped into a chair.

"Whew. That's done. It's like a furnace in that barn."

"I'll pour up the milk," said Mama. "Why dinna you sit and rest a bit. Mary, fetch me the pans. Charlotte, you go on readin'."

Charlotte scanned the inky page for more items of interest. Suddenly she gasped and cried out, "Mama! Listen to this!"

But she was so interested by the headline that she forgot to read aloud, until Mama teased her. Then she read, tripping over the words in her excitement:

## New School for Young Ladies in Roxbury

BETSY EATON *respectfully informs her friends and patrons that she will commence a School in Warren Street, for the instruction of Young Ladies in the following useful and ornamental branches of Education.*

*Reading, Writing, Arithmetic, English Grammar, French Language, Composition, Geography, Use of the Globe and Maps, Embroidery, Tambour, Plain and Ornamental Needlework, Drawing and Painting in a superior style, in oils, crayons, water-colours, &c. Painting on velvet, drawing and colouring Maps.*

*Fees made known on application. Instruction to commence on the 22nd of June, for a four months' term.*

"Oh, Mama!" cried Lydia. "May we go?"

"Yes, *please* say we may go!" Charlotte

pleaded. She wasn't sure why she was so excited. Maybe it was because the school sounded elegant. She wanted to learn to draw and paint in a superior style in oils, crayons, and watercolors, though she was none too sure exactly what those things were.

Mama looked troubled.

"I dinna ken," she said slowly. "I'll have to talk to your papa about this. We dinna ken aught about this Betsy Eaton, to start wi', and then who kens how much she aims to charge? I'm not sayin' nay outright," she added, seeing their crestfallen faces, "but I dinna wish to rush in wi' an 'aye' when there's a great many questions to be answered afore I can give you so much as a 'perhaps.'"

She sighed, lifting one of the heavy milk pans to carry it to the larder.

"Besides, I'd miss you if you went away all day. And when the—"

She cut her words short and disappeared into the larder. Charlotte and Lydia looked at each other. Charlotte knew in a glance that Lydia was just as keen to go to Miss Eaton's school as she was. Lydia had never cared much for her studies when she used to go to school. She had been glad to grow too old for it. But Miss Eaton's school did not sound much like the little Roxbury village school Charlotte and Lydia had gone to when they were younger. They had not studied drawing and painting and tambour (whatever that was) and French.

Charlotte had liked the village school just fine, most of the time. But she was growing too old for it now. Few girls continued at school past eleven or twelve years of age. Few boys did either, for that matter. Tom was unusual in wanting to continue his studies. Papa intended to enroll him in the Roxbury Latin School next term, which would begin in September, after the busy harvesttime.

Tom was thirteen now, old enough to be apprenticed somewhere. Everyone in the family knew he did not want to apprentice in Papa's shop but was too loyal to say so. Everyone also knew that Papa was talking to other tradesmen, looking for a place where Tom might learn a trade he would enjoy while meeting with good treatment from the master. Some masters were cruel to their apprentices. In the meantime, Papa was willing to let him continue at school.

Charlotte had gone to the town school last winter and looked forward to a spring and summer free from studying. But now the vision of Miss Eaton's School for Young Ladies rose appealingly before her eyes. In the space of one minute she had gone from having no idea such a school existed to yearning for it with her whole heart and soul. Lydia's hands were clasped with the same yearning. Mama and Papa *must* say yes!

While she and Lydia were exchanging hopeful glances, Mary was looking back and forth between them, hands on her hips.

"Will I go too?" she demanded. "How old do you have to be for this school?"

"Oh, you're much too little," said Lydia. Charlotte winced, knowing the storm that was coming.

"I'm not!" cried Mary, her eyes flashing. "Let me see that paper. Does it say aught about how old you must be?"

Charlotte handed it over reluctantly, feeling a stab of guilt. She knew without asking that Mary was too young for such a school. The newspaper said "School for Young Ladies." Charlotte was a little worried that Miss Eaton might not accept eleven-year-olds.

Even if Miss Eaton accepted girls as young as Mary, Charlotte knew there was no way Mama would let her go. She would need someone home to help with the chores, and—

The baby. Charlotte had forgotten about the baby that was coming. She wished she knew when Mama expected it to arrive. Surely there were at least four months to go. It was hard to tell under Mama's loose, high-waisted gown exactly how big her belly was, but Charlotte was sure that Lucy's had been a great deal bigger before Anna was born.

# *The Secret Sorrow*

**M**ama's grave eyes warned against further discussion of the subject that evening. All through supper Charlotte and Lydia dared not look at each other, for fear their longing would announce itself.

Later that evening, when Charlotte slipped downstairs for a drink of water before bed, she heard Mama and Papa talking in the parlor about the school. Mama sounded upset and . . . confused. This puzzled Charlotte. She wouldn't have been surprised if Mama had said no about the school, plain and simple. "No, we canna afford it," or "No, I need you at home." Mama was unflinchingly direct, and whether or not you agreed with her reasons for something, you knew where she stood. But it seemed to Charlotte, frozen in the short passageway at the foot of the stairs, that on this question Mama herself did not know where she stood.

"I canna for the life o' me understand why they'd want to go. I ken what that school will be like. A lot o' mincing, giggling girls gossiping about who has the sweetest frock and whose hair is thickest. Whisht, I'd sooner join the army than spend another term in such a place."

"Ye canna be certain 'twill be the same sort o' school as yours was. 'Tis worth lookin' into, Martha. Charlotte's a bright lass. Happen 'twill be just the thing for her. Geography and French, think o' it!"

"Aye, and seven kinds o' fancywork I could teach her meself, and the eminently practical art o' painting blurry landscapes on second-rate velvet!" Mama's voice was icy with scorn.

Papa only laughed; he was never cross with Mama.

Charlotte suddenly realized she was eaves-dropping, and close upon that guilty revela-tion came a rush of panic lest she should be caught. She crept back up the stairs as silently as she could. The old plank stairs creaked a little, but Mama's urgent voice covered the noise. Lydia and Mary were already in bed. Charlotte knelt and said her prayers with con-siderable emphasis on the "forgive us our trespasses" part. She had not meant to tres-pass on her parents' conversation, but neither had she hurried away.

"What's taking you so long?" Mary whis-pered.

"Shhh! Can't you see I'm praying?" asked Charlotte virtuously. She remained kneeling a moment longer to show that a true penitent must not be rushed—though all prayerful thoughts, peninent or otherwise, had been chased from her head by Mary's interruption. She rose from her knees and climbed over

Mary into her spot in the middle of the bed. Lydia scooted over to make room for her, murmuring a sleepy good night.

Charlotte lay awake a long time, her mind roiling with the things she had heard. There was something about Mama she did not understand. Mama was the merriest, most talkative mother Charlotte knew. Other mothers she had met were quiet or weary or cross, or some combination of the three. Mama liked lively discussions and boisterous teasing and dramatic storytelling. She herself was the best storyteller Charlotte had ever heard. She often wished the schoolmaster had Mama's knack for spinning a tale. Sometimes when Charlotte complained about a dull history lesson, Mama would tell the story herself and bring it vividly to life with her ringing voice and blazing eyes.

And yet she seldom told the stories of her own life. When she did tell one, it was usually because Papa had coaxed it out of her. Charlotte was sure there must be heaps of tales Mama could tell about her growing-up

days, if she but chose to. It perplexed
Charlotte that Mama could be so . . . so open,
and yet so closed. School, for example—had
Mama really attended a school for young
ladies? Why had she never talked about it? Was
it a day school or had she boarded somewhere
away from home? How old had she been?
Evidently she had not much liked it. But why?

Charlotte knew her mother had had a
happy childhood. That much she had gathered from the snippets of tales Papa had
teased out of Mama over the years. What's
more, she had been someone important; her
father had been a kind of lord. Charlotte did
not know much about lords, except the ones
in *Ivanhoe*, which Mama had at last begun to
read to the family. A thrill ran up Charlotte's
spine—somehow she had never given it
much thought before. Her own grandfather, a
lord like the Saxon chief Cedric! Only *Ivanhoe*
was set in England, not Scotland, and hundreds of years ago, when there were knights
and Crusades and jousting tournaments.
Mama's childhood could not have been quite

like that. Mama had said once that her
father's house was not even as large as the
Dudley mansion near Roxbury Common.
Charlotte could not understand how a
Scottish lord could have a house less grand
than that of an ordinary (albeit rich) towns-
man of no noble descent.

And Mama! She ought to be clad in silk and
gold like Lady Rowena, the Saxon princess!
She ought to have a houseful of servants waiting on her, instead of having to do all kinds of
heavy, messy work herself. Surely she had not
been brought up to do housework. And yet
she never complained; indeed, she sang and
talked as she went about her work. Why, she
almost seemed to enjoy it! Charlotte's heart
swelled with sudden pride in her mother, who
put on such a brave and cheerful face when
she must be secretly chafing against her life
of toil and servitude. Mama loved Papa so
fiercely, she would never want to hurt him by
complaining. Perhaps she didn't like to talk
about her childhood for fear of rubbing Papa's
nose in the things he was not able to give

her—jewels, servants, walls hung with silk and tapestries.

Perhaps—Charlotte gasped into the stifling darkness, causing Mary to stir beside her— perhaps that was why Mama had reacted so strongly against the idea of her daughters attending a school where they would be taught art and music and French. Maybe Mama felt her own education was wasted, and she did not want Charlotte and Lydia to suffer a similar disappointment.

A strange wave of feeling came over Charlotte. She felt sorry for Mama and almost protective of her. It was uncomfortable to feel sorry for Mama. She seemed such a jolly, hearty person, the last sort of person you would ever think carried a secret sorrow within her heart.

Charlotte made a silent resolution. She would protect Mama's secret. She would do nothing to cause her pain. She would never, ever mention Miss Betsy Eaton's school again.

So she was surprised the next morning when Mama greeted Charlotte and Lydia with a calm smile and the words: "Papa and I have decided. We'll look into Miss Eaton's qualifications, and if we're satisfied wi' her character and her terms, we'll enroll you both. For one term only, mind, and after that we'll have to see."

# First Church of Roxbury

Charlotte couldn't wait for church that week. These days she saw her friends only on Sundays, between the morning and afternoon meetings. Now that she knew she might be—probably was—going to Miss Eaton's school, she was frantic to know whether her best friend, Ellie Till, would be allowed to go too. It would not be half so much fun if Ellie weren't there.

The heat had not let up. It was too hot to close the meetinghouse doors during the sermon. The Reverend Dr. Porter, in his heavy black robe, clutched the pulpit with both hands as if it were the only thing keeping him on his feet. His broad face gleamed with perspiration; droplets trickled down from his forehead and quivered in bright beads on his nose. He mopped repeatedly at his face with a crisp new handkerchief. His initials were embroidered in the corner in turkey red, and as the sermon wore on, Charlotte noticed that whoever had sold Mrs. Porter that thread had not made the dye fast. Slowly the elegant, curving, turkey-red EP (for Eliphalet Porter) spread red tendrils into the white linen. A swipe across the forehead, and the EP was a red smudge. Charlotte held her breath, wondering if soon the dye would begin to come off on Dr. Porter's skin. It was fortunate that it was red dye—it matched Dr. Porter's heat-flushed face.

Charlotte knew she shouldn't be thinking of such things in church. She sat very still, squeezed in between Mary and Tom. Mama kept putting a hand on Mary's knee to stop her from swinging her legs. Tom squirmed uncomfortably, tugging at his stiff collar. Papa eyed him without turning his head. All around Charlotte were the rustlings and sighs of a congregation slowly roasting alive. Small children scooted close to their mothers to benefit from the feeble breeze raised by painted fans. Someone's dog wandered in from the common, and one of the elders shooed it back out. Somewhere behind Charlotte a little boy laughed out loud—presumably about the dog. Three sharp steps rang on the floorboards; Charlotte was wincing even before the crack of an elder's switch snapped through the hush. A muffled yelp, a hissed *Shhh*, and then silence. The heavy footfalls retreated to the back of the church.

There were four elders, known to the children of the congregation as tappers. They paced the aisles on silent feet, clasping long willow switches behind their backs, alert for the slightest hint of a giggle or whisper. Charlotte had never been tapped. She fervently hoped she never would be. *Tap* was hardly the word to describe the energetic blows she had so often heard the tappers deal out. Papa's pew was close to the front of the church, so Charlotte had not seen many people tapped—not since she was very small, when Lewis was a young boy. Mama said that back in the day, if a Sunday meeting passed without a tap or two for Lewis, she would know he was coming down with something and she'd better take him home and put him straight to bed.

Dr. Porter was reading a passage from the Bible about the Israelites wandering in the desert for forty years. Charlotte wondered if their desert had been as hot as this meeting-house. She doubted it was possible.

Ever since the anonymous vandals had destroyed the parish Bible, Dr. Porter had read his texts from his own well-worn copy of the scriptures. For three weeks he strode to the pulpit clutching that Bible close to his chest, as if protecting it from unseen attackers who might leap out from behind a pew, wielding scissors or flame. But in all this time he had never said a word from the pulpit about the destruction of the beautiful old Bible that had belonged to the First Church of Roxbury for over fifty years. Papa said the identity of the vandals had never been determined, and probably never would be, unless someone confessed to it. And that, everyone agreed, was unlikely to happen.

But after the sermon today Dr. Porter made an announcement. He was beaming with pleasure. The esteemed Mr. Samuel Gardner, he said, was donating a new Bible to the church. It had already been ordered from a merchant in Boston and was expected to arrive within the week. Mr. Gardner's generosity was an act of goodness as great in proportion as the wickedness of the depraved soul or souls who had wreaked destruction on the original.

All heads turned to smile at the generous Mr. Gardner, who stood blushing in the back of the meetinghouse. He was one of the elders, a stout, respectable man who made clocks. Charlotte had seen him often among the men in her father's smithy. He was reputed to wield his willow switch with more force than any other tapper.

Charlotte could not imagine who would be so wicked as to destroy a Bible. The idea that anyone in Roxbury would be capable of such a thing—why, it was unthinkable! Unless . . . she recalled what old Seneca Harrington had said about the shiftless, drunken, lazy quarrymen on Papa's stone ledge. Why, you would almost have to be drunk to commit such a wicked crime, wouldn't you? She shuddered. To think of those men working on her father's own land. She had probably seen them passing her house. Suppose they took it into their wicked heads to enter the Tucker home one night and slash up *their* Bible? Or murder them in their beds?

She was so intent upon these frightening visions that it was like coming out of a dream to stand and sing the closing hymn.

*Lord, dismiss us with Thy blessing;*
*Fill our hearts with joy and peace;*
*Let us each Thy love possessing,*

*Triumph in redeeming grace.*
*O refresh us, O refresh us,*
*Traveling through this wilderness.*

Everyone rose and shuffled out of the hot, stifling meetinghouse to the hot, stifling out-of-doors. It was worse outside with the sun beating down through hats and bonnets. Nonetheless, the churchgoers lingered in the road, talking—about the weather mostly. There was no reason to hurry home; nowhere would there be relief from the terrible heat.

Charlotte hunted the crowd for Ellie Till. Ellie found her first.

"Charlotte! Have you heard about Miss Eaton's school?"

"Aye, I'm going! At least, I think I am. Are you? Oh, I hope you are," gasped Charlotte.

Ellie was going. She said her mother was vastly pleased with the notion.

"She was thinking of sending me to a seminary in Boston in a year or two, or to Miss Saunders's school in Dorchester. But I'd have had to board. It's cheaper if I stay home."

Charlotte shrugged. "Who'd want to board anyway? Wouldn't you miss your family dreadfully?"

"Miss Eaton's taking boarders," said Ellie. "Ma says she has six pupils already. Eight, counting you and me. Is Lydia going?"

Charlotte nodded.

"Then that makes nine. I wonder if Freda Gregg will go."

"What do you suppose Miss Eaton is like?" Charlotte asked.

"Why, didn't you see her in church?" asked Ellie. "She was right behind you, in Mr. Abel Dillaway's pew. The tall, skinny lady with the rosettes on her bonnet."

"Her?" Charlotte was surprised. "Why, I've seen her before, lots of times."

"Of course you have. She's Emma Dillaway's cousin. You know Miss Dillaway, don't you?"

"I should say I do!" Charlotte and Lydia had been secretly observing pretty Miss Dillaway for months. They had noticed how the color rushed up into her face whenever Lewis spoke to her, and Lewis, always so teasing and self-assured, became courteous and soft-spoken in her presence, as if he were trying to imitate Papa. Lydia said Lewis was smitten with Miss Dillaway.

"He's going to court her, you watch and see," she had told Charlotte. Ever since, Charlotte had been watching Lewis and Miss Dillaway like a hawk.

"Well," continued Ellie, "Miss Eaton's mother is Mrs. Dillaway's sister. She lives in that house on Warren Street next to the milliner's shop, you know the one. Miss Eaton used to keep house for her brother over in Brookline, but he's getting married, so she's coming back here to live with her mother. The school is going to be in their house."

Charlotte felt a little deflated. She had pictured Miss Betsy Eaton as a beautiful, sophisticated, elegant lady from Boston who rode to Sunday meeting in a coach and four. And there she was standing in the dusty road with Mrs. Samuel Waitt, droplets of perspiration beading her upper lip. Charlotte would not have supposed that the mistress of a school for young ladies could sweat. It seemed indelicate.

Forgetting that it was just as indelicate to stare, Charlotte stood watching Miss Eaton as she exchanged pleasantries with other ladies.

The schoolmistress was tall and thin indeed, with a long, handsome, animated face. She moved her hands whenever she spoke. It could not be denied that her dress was fashionable, even if she was from Brookline. It was made of a pale-blue linen, with short, tight sleeves and a square neckline embroidered with golden vines. A golden sash ran directly under the bodice, and the skirt was straight and graceful. More golden vines twined along the hem. Charlotte studied the delicate embroidery appreciatively. *I'd like to make a gown like that*, she thought.

Ellie's mother called her. She said good-bye and hurried off. Charlotte saw Mama move toward Miss Eaton and Mrs. Waitt. Quickly Charlotte ducked away, afraid Mama would summon her to be introduced to the schoolmistress. She did not want to meet Miss Eaton like this, hot and sweaty in the middle of the road. She slipped around the corner of the meetinghouse, where there was a sliver of feeble shade.

She was not alone. What she saw was a strange sight that made her shrink back in surprise. A man was leaning against the church, his hands pressed to his face as if he were crying or in pain. Charlotte could not see his face, but she knew by his clothes who he was. It was Mr. Samuel Gardner, the man who had donated the Bible.

Charlotte did not want him to know he had been seen. But when she backed quietly away, a twig cracked under her shoe. His face shot up, and he stared at her with wild, dismayed eyes.

Then he snapped, "What are you looking at?"

"N-nothing," Charlotte stammered. "I'm sorry. I didn't know anyone was here."

Mr. Gardner's voice softened. "You ought

to go home, young lady. This heat'll make you sick."

He turned and strode quickly away toward the common.

Charlotte was quiet all the walk home. She could not forget the anguish she had seen on Mr. Gardner's face.

# *The Lady-in-Waiting*

E ver since that night on the stairs, Charlotte had felt protective of Mama. And the farther the family got in *Ivanhoe*, the more Charlotte ached for the absent grandeur and luxury she believed her mother was entitled to. She winced at the sight of Mama's rough, work-reddened hands. Those hands should be lily white, holding bouquets of flowers instead of brooms and fireplace tongs.

One night a thought came to Charlotte with a thrill up her spine. *She* would be Mama's servant. She would be like one of Lady Rowena's ladies-in-waiting to her beautiful, brave, queenly mother, so patiently bearing the sad twist of fortune that had reduced her from her high station. That the "sad twist of fortune" was her marriage to Papa, who was unquestionably the dearest, kindest, best man in the entire world, was a contradiction Charlotte brushed out of her mind as inconsequential. It was a cruelty of fate that Papa had not been born a nobleman. Charlotte resolved to make up for it.

She began at once. She got up very early the next morning, before anyone else was up, and crept down to the kitchen with her dress over her arm. She did not want to risk waking her sisters by getting dressed in the bedchamber. She went out to the lean-to to shrug into her frock, and with a carelessness unlike her usual neat, precise movements, she swiped a comb once or twice through her hair and tied it away from her face with an old frayed ribbon. Servant girls needn't take much trouble with their appearance. Charlotte had not quite made clear in her mind whether she was lowly drudge or demure lady-in-waiting, and had settled vaguely for some combination of the two.

With brisk efficiency she set to work readying the coals for the breakfast fire, hauling in water, measuring spoonfuls of loose tea into the teapot. Her diligence was rewarded, for when Mama appeared in the doorway, her hair still hanging in a long braid down her back beneath a lacy nightcap, she blinked in wonder and then bestowed a radiant smile upon Charlotte.

"Why, Lottie! Aren't you the busy lass this mornin'? Sure and you've done half my work for me already!"

That was the nicest thing she could have said. Charlotte beamed at her, saying eagerly, "The water's almost ready for tea, Mama. Sit down—I'll pour you a cup."

Mama looked at her curiously. "Thank you, love, but I've got to go back and get dressed. I only came out to stir up the coals. Which you've already done, you darling." She kissed

Charlotte's cheek. "Seeing as you're dressed already, why dinna you run out for a ramble before breakfast? Sure and you've earned it."

Charlotte shook her head and smiled indulgently at her mother. "You go on back, Mama. I mean ma'am. I'll bring you your tea when it's ready."

Mama's expression had moved from curious to perplexed. Charlotte held back a giggle. Probably Mama did not know what to make of her sudden shift in fortunes. At last she would be given the leisurely morning she deserved. Charlotte fairly danced with pride. With a last bewildered glance Mama went back to her bedroom.

When she returned, washed and dressed, Charlotte was waiting, poised and alert, watchful for any little thing she could do to relieve her mother's burden of work. All morning, much to Mary's annoyance, she hovered at Mama's side, rushing to carry what must be carried, or stir what must be stirred, or sweep what must be swept. Mary wanted Charlotte to go outside and play, but Charlotte could not be persuaded. Mary gave up on her in disgust and went to visit the sheep in the back meadow.

If Lydia noticed anything unusual about Charlotte's behavior, she didn't comment. She was absorbed in finishing a new dress in time for the opening of Miss Eaton's school. The term was to begin the following week.

When Mama sat down to mend a tear in Tom's second-best pants, Charlotte swooped in with a bouquet of roses she had kept in waiting.

"Here, let me do the mending, Mama!"

"Are you feelin' quite well, Lottie?" Mama joked. "I fear you're comin' down wi' some mysterious ailment. I'll have to look o'er me herbs and see if I have a cure."

"No, ma'am, I'm quite well, thank you, ma'am."

Mama laughed until tears came to her eyes when Charlotte asked if she might dress her hair. She seemed to look upon Charlotte's behavior as a delightful sort of joke, though Charlotte remained earnest and serious in her servitude throughout the forenoon.

But when she leaped in front of Mama on the way back from the henhouse to brush a stick from her path, Mama burst out in irritation.

"Whatever are you playin' at, Lottie? You'll make me break these eggs if you dinna look out."

Charlotte's face fell. "I'm sorry, ma'am! I didn't mean to cause you trouble, ma'am. Why, that's the last thing I wanted!"

"And that's another thing. It's been 'ma'am' this and 'ma'am' that all day. I canna make out what's come over you."

Charlotte didn't answer. She stared at the ground, feeling foolish and disappointed.

Mama's gentle hand lifted her chin.

"You need to tell me what's goin' on," she said, her voice soft and kind.

Charlotte's eyes filled with tears.

"I was only trying to help you," she said. "You have so much work, and it isn't right. You ought to be sitting on a cushion, eating strawberries and cream."

Mama drew in a sudden breath.

"Ah. I think I understand." Her green eyes twinkled into Charlotte's. "I think you've guessed that I'm expectin' a baby. Haven't you?"

"Oh, I've known that for ages," said Charlotte. "A month at least."

Mama drew back in surprise, laughter bubbling out of her. "Och, you have, have you? Well, now. A whole month. Why, then, is it only today you've decided to take my work upon your shoulders?"

Charlotte picked at a loose thread in her apron, fumbling to put her swirling thoughts into words.

"I . . . I'm sorry for you, Mama! You weren't brought up to a life of toil and drudgery. Your father was a lord! You ought to be clad in sea-green silk like the Lady Rowena, and be crowned the Queen of Love and Beauty at tournaments and things!"

Mama laughed so hard, she had to set the basket of eggs upon the ground.

"Tournaments!" she exclaimed.

"Well, if they had tournaments around here, I mean. At the very least you ought to have a houseful of servants like Mrs. Ebenezer Craft, and ride to meeting in a coach and four." She clutched her mother's hands. "You weren't born to this life."

"Lottie." Mama's laughter had quieted but it was still there brimming in her eyes. "Not born to this life! Why, I'm the most fortunate woman ever lived! Do you ken where I spent my childhood? In the kitchen, wi' my mother's servants. I loved it there, wi' all the bustle and chatter and the fine smells comin' out o' Cook's pots. I used to beg Cook to let me help. I could see they worked hard, the servants did, wi' precious little rest, but it was good work, important work, feedin' a family, keepin' the house trim, makin' our home a pleasant place to be. My mother treated her servants wi' respect, for she kenned how much we relied on them."

She squeezed Charlotte's hands. "It's proud I am to serve my own family by keepin' my own house now, Charlotte. 'Tis a gift to me, you ken. God granted the wish o' my heart. To be sure, I get weary sometimes, and there's tasks I dinna relish, like makin' soap. But even then, I'm that grateful to have a houseful o' dirty hands to make soap *for*."

Charlotte laughed. A blacksmith's wife certainly did encounter a vast number of dirty hands.

But Mama grew serious. "Dinna you dare pity me," she said. "'Tis an insult to your father. And to me, for that matter. There's naught to pity me for. I'd not trade places wi' Lady Rowena for all the sea-green silk in China."

Charlotte nodded solemnly. She remembered suddenly that even Lady Rowena had not lived in the perfect comfort befitting Charlotte's notion of a princess. Mama had read of the rich silken tapestries adorning her walls—and the icy drafts that blew through the crevices so sharply that the torch flames streamed out sideways.

She followed Mama across the yard, seeing anew the snug walls of their trim clapboard house. Charlotte loved that house. She loved the neat square rooms, the parlor wallpaper with its garlands of roses, the crowded kitchen with bundles of herbs hanging from the ceiling. She loved knowing which steps squeaked in the staircase that led up to the two small bedchambers.

The dwellings in *Ivanhoe* tended to be large, chilly places with lots of dogs running around eating scraps from the floor. There wasn't a castle in the whole book she'd like to live in, not even Prince John's. Not one of them could hold a candle to her own nice house on Tide Mill Lane.

# The School for
# Young Ladies

The rest of that week was spent in a
flurry of getting ready for Miss Eaton's
school. Mama helped Charlotte make
a new frock; Lydia's was almost finished.
Charlotte did all the cutting herself, and a good
deal of the sewing. Mama said she herself was
no match for Charlotte when it came to making
a straight seam.

Charlotte's dress was a rosy red calico
sprigged with white flowers. Lydia's was a

dark green just the color of a pine tree. There was enough fabric left from Charlotte's dress to make a matching one for Mary. Mary was delighted; she seldom got a dress that had not been worn by at least one of her sisters.

Lydia was lively with excitement and even more absentminded than usual. Mama teased Lydia for her scatterbrained ways, joking that it was a wonder her seams didn't run in zigzags instead of straight lines, so often was Lydia's gaze turned upward at her castles in the air instead of down at her needle. It was only teasing, for somehow Lydia's seams did come out straight and her chores got done, no matter how far afield her thoughts drifted while she did them.

She had Mama's own gift for storytelling. Charlotte loved to hear her sister's stories; often as they worked side by side in the garden, Lydia entertained her with some fanciful tale of romance and valor—all the more romantic and valorous since Mama had begun reading *Ivanhoe*.

Charlotte thought her sister was lovely,

with her silky golden hair and luminous eyes. She had been shocked to the core at a cornhusking last fall to hear Mrs. Caleb Baldwin remark to Mrs. John Mason that it was a pity the oldest Tucker girl had such a plain face under all that yellow hair.

"Ah well," Mrs. Mason had sighed. "It's right pretty hair, though."

Charlotte had quivered with indignant fury. Why, anyone could see that Lydia was beautiful! Her eyes sparkled like candlelight when she spoke, and she moved with the easy grace of a leaf fluttering to the ground.

When Lydia put on her new school dress, Charlotte thought she was more beautiful than ever. The rich piney calico brought a green tint to her eyes and a warmth to her fair skin. It had a waist as high as a waist could possibly be, then fell in soft folds to the floor. The sleeves were short and slightly puffed, and the square neckline was edged with a dark-green ribbon. Lydia looked so grown-up that Charlotte felt almost shy. But when she tried on the rosy calico and saw how gracefully it draped to her ankles, she felt grown-up too.

She felt considerably less confident on the morning she stood beside Lydia outside the door of Miss Betsy Eaton's house on Warren Street. It was a long walk from home—up Tide Mill Lane to Washington Street, and along Washington past the meetinghouse and the town common, all the way to Warren Street near the Neck. Lydia, looking bright and eager in her new straw bonnet with a black satin ribbon, rapped the door knocker. She gave Charlotte's hand a squeeze but dropped it when the door began to open.

They were greeted by a soft-voiced, gray-haired woman in a sober brown dress. This was Mrs. Eaton, Miss Betsy Eaton's mother. Charlotte recognized her from Sunday meeting. She welcomed them inside to a sitting room papered with a pattern of creamy bouquets on a white ground. Lace-edged ivory-colored curtains hung in the windows, and the floor was covered with a woven carpet with green and blue stripes. The room was full of chairs and girls, but none of the girls were sitting. Charlotte saw Ellie Till at once, and Freda Gregg, and some older girls she knew from church. Lydia went to stand with them. Everyone was whispery and nervous, waiting for Miss Eaton.

"Should we sit down?" Charlotte murmured to Ellie.

"I don't know," Ellie whispered back.

They heard footsteps in the hall, and Miss Eaton came in. Today she was wearing a pretty pelisse dress made of green-and-white striped linen. Her hair was parted in the middle, with many soft ringlets around her face; the rest was coiled into a knot at the back of her head.

"Good morning, young ladies," said Miss Eaton, and that was the beginning of school. She gestured toward the chairs that made a wide half circle in the middle of the room and told them that from now on they must take their seats when they came in, and rise to greet her when she entered. With a quiet shuffling, the girls found seats. Charlotte was between Ellie and Freda. Lydia was at the far end of the half circle next to a plump, merry-eyed girl name Sadie Baxter. Sadie had a younger brother who had been in Charlotte's class at the village school years ago.

Miss Eaton began the day with morning prayers and introductions. Three of her students, she explained, lived too far away to be day scholars. They would board with Miss Eaton and her mother. The girl named Susannah seemed about Charlotte and Ellie's age; Sarah and Eunice were a little older. Besides Charlotte and Lydia, there were four other day scholars: Ellie, Freda, Sadie, and another girl of fourteen or fifteen who was, Charlotte knew, a niece of Mrs. Samuel Waitt. Her name was Phebe Southwell, and Charlotte had met her many times at the Waitt house.

It was strange to see Phebe here, her hair carefully twisted up, her hands folded on her lap, listening to Miss Eaton with polite attention. Charlotte remembered chasing Mrs. Waitt's chickens with Phebe once, long ago, and the dreadful scolding Mrs. Waitt had given them afterward. Phebe's hair had been falling out of two loose braids then, and her petticoats always showed below her skirt. Now she was a young lady, like Lydia. *Like me,* Charlotte reminded herself. They were all young ladies now, learning to do young-lady things, and for an instant Charlotte had a sense of something she could not put into words—a feeling that Miss Eaton's parlor was a place somehow removed from the rest of the world. Outside, little girls ran after exasperated chickens in sunny barnyards. In here, the morning sun filtered gracefully through crisp lace-edged curtains, and Miss Eaton's gentle voice talked about the privilege and adventure of education.

That first day set the pattern for all the days at Miss Eaton's school. Morning prayers in the sitting room, hymn singing, and then the girls took out their tambour frames and workbaskets. The mysterious and alluring "tambour" mentioned in Miss Eaton's advertisement turned out to be a fancy name for embroidery. The background fabric was held taut in a wooden frame of a sort that Charlotte had seen hundreds of times in her life, in dozens of parlors all over Roxbury. She just hadn't known its proper name was "tambour frame." Miss Eaton said it was named after a kind of drum.

She gave the girls the assignment of copying a piece of fine needlework she had done. It was a family record sampler, with rows of cross-stitched names and birthdates in the center, framed by a wide border of flowers and vines. Below the family names in the center panel were two beautifully embroidered pear trees flanking a blue-and-white basket heaped with flowers. Charlotte thought Miss Eaton's sampler was a marvelous piece of work, the creamy linen background set off by delicate shades of coral, rose, sky blue, and green, with a much-embellished signature beneath the basket of flowers:

*Elizabeth A. Eaton, 1820*

Miss Eaton distributed pieces of linen to put in the tambour frames, and she showed the girls how to mark the correct point at which to begin cross-stitching the title:

## FAMILY RECORD

Below that, each girl was to stitch the names of her father and mother, with their birthdates, and the date of their wedding on the next line down.

*Mr Lewis Tucker born Aug$^{st}$ 18$^{th}$ 1780*

*Miss Martha Morse born Jan 1$^{st}$ 1782*

*Married Jan 1$^{st}$ 1799*

During that first week, as the words began to take shape beneath her needle, Charlotte could not help but feel a little thrill of pride. The names looked so neat and crisp, emblazoned there in a straight—well, *almost* straight—line for all the world to see. She could not wait to move through the list of her older siblings to her own name. Ellie and Freda were eager to move on to the bright, elaborate flowers of the border, but Charlotte thought the names were the best part. It was funny to think of her name appearing on Lydia's sampler, and Lydia's on hers. Charlotte knew Mary would be tickled to see her name on both samplers, proud and important at the bottom of the list. She would have to remember to leave room at the bottom for the baby Mama was expecting. What fun, to know that there was a space already marked out for a little person whose name she didn't know yet. Boy or girl—dark-blue thread or scarlet? The mystery was as interesting as the sampler.

During the needlework hour one girl was chosen each day to read aloud to the others. Sometimes it was the poetry of William Cullen Bryant or Mrs. Lydia Sigourney; sometimes it was weighty passages from a book of sermons.

"For your interest and instruction," Miss Eaton explained—more instructive than interesting, Charlotte thought, on days when Sarah Huggins or Freda Gregg droned on and on.

After needlework, the girls moved to a rather stuffy room in the back of the house that had been equipped with two rows of tables. There they studied geography and arithmetic, working out their problems on slates. They copied passages of poetry into homemade copybooks, while Miss Eaton walked behind them, tapping their shoulders to remind them to keep their backs straight. Miss Eaton was extremely particular about the proper position in which to sit while writing.

"One must keep one's shoulders quite even and back perfectly straight," she insisted, demonstrating with her own impeccable posture. Freda Gregg, Miss Eaton declared, was troubled with an unfortunate inclination to lean to the left. To correct this handicap, Freda was made to write with a book underneath her left elbow.

"If this fails," said Miss Eaton ruefully, "we

shall have to place a book upon your head. In order to prevent it from falling, you will have to hold your back perfectly rigid. I think it will correct the problem quite expediently."

Freda shuddered, and the other girls shuddered with her. Some of Miss Eaton's ideas were decidedly uncomfortable.

"One must maintain an elegant pen-holding position by gracefully curving the wrist," Miss Eaton would say. "Writing should be fluid and flawless, as if the ink pours directly from one's hand onto the page without the clumsy intrusion of a pen."

Whenever Miss Eaton talked in that way, Charlotte had to restrain herself from glancing at Ellie or Lydia. She liked Miss Eaton, truly she did, but she could not help but wonder if certain things were *quite* as important as Miss Eaton insisted they were. She could imagine how Mama would snort with scorn if she were there. Sometimes she felt like snorting herself.

But she liked Miss Eaton's school. She liked the companionable chatter over dinner in the

Eatons' pretty dining room. She liked the afternoon painting lessons and writing compositions about subjects like patriotism and courage. She liked being able to annoy her brothers by peppering her speeches with phrases of French. (Tom retaliated by answering back in Latin, but Charlotte only shrugged unconcernedly and said he'd better enjoy it while he could, for next year Miss Eaton was going to start them on Virgil.) She loved being part of a group of girls who knew each other better and better as the weeks went by. She felt closer to Lydia than ever; the gap of four years between them seemed narrower now that they were learning French and tambour together.

# *Mack*

The summer fell into a routine of hot walks across town to Miss Eaton's, busy days of lessons in the lacy sitting room and the stuffy classroom, and hot walks home in the afternoon. In the mornings Mary walked with them as far as Mr. Waitt's mill, for she was attending the summer term at the village school. Charlotte felt a pang of guilt every time she watched Mary go off alone down the dusty road that led to the small one-room schoolhouse. She knew Mary would have gone alone this summer no matter what—Charlotte was much too old for the summer school. But she felt guilty just the same. Mary would look back over her shoulder and wave wistfully at Charlotte and Lydia, her dinner basket swinging on her arm. She looked so little to be going by herself. But she was seven now, and that was old enough.

The girls were in the kitchen, tying each other's hair ribbons, and Mama was just ladling thick oatmeal porridge onto plates, when a neighbor boy rushed into the house, breathless, tracking mud on the floor. It was Johnny Waitt, the miller's son.

"Ma sent me," he panted. "You're needed quick, Mrs. Tucker. A lady fell into the mill pond."

"What?" gasped Mama, already reaching for her bonnet. "Lydia, you come too. Charlotte, mind the sausage."

"What about school?" Charlotte gasped.

"Never mind school. Stay here for now."

They were gone in a dizzying blur, leaving Charlotte and Mary to stare at each other in wonder. Charlotte collected her wits.

"We ought to tell Papa," she said. He had gone over to the smithy to start the fire in the forge, as he did every morning. The boys were feeding the livestock. Mary went outside, hollering for Lewis before her feet had crossed the threshold. Charlotte stood at the window watching Mary chatter to her brothers in the barnyard. Then Tom took off toward the smithy, and Lewis went back to the barn.

Charlotte paced the kitchen, feeling desperate to know what was happening. Who had fallen into the pond? Had she drowned?

Mary came inside. "I want to go see. Can't we go?"

"Ohhh," said Charlotte, sorely tempted. She felt half mad with curiosity. But her conscience was shouting at her in a stern voice. She sighed reluctantly. "No, we'd better not. Mama said to stay. I suppose we ought to go ahead and eat breakfast."

Mary gave a little stomp of frustration. Charlotte set about scraping all but three of the dishes of porridge back into the pot to keep warm. She made sure the pot was close but not too close to the fire, so that the porridge would stay warm but not burn. She was just turning the sausages in the iron skillet, wondering if she and Lydia would go to school at all that day, when there came a knock on the door.

For a moment she thought it must be Johnny Waitt again, but then she remembered that he had not knocked the first time; he had just barged in. And he had come in through the lean-to, as the family always did. Whoever had knocked had done so at the seldom-used front door. A stranger, then.

She opened the door cautiously, half fearing to see one of the drunken quarrymen she had heard such frightful things about.

"Why, it's you!" she cried in surprise.

The person on the doorstep laughed. It was the nice surveyor man she and Mary had talked to on the road in June. He looked as boyish as Tom, smiling at them with his half-moon eyes, the wind ruffling the hair beneath his cap. Charlotte noticed with some alarm that he was clutching what looked like a blood-stained handkerchief in one hand.

But the man was smiling. "I spoke to your brother in the barnyard," he said. "He told me I might come in and beg a bandage of you. Cut my hand, I did, while I was setting up my equipment."

"Oh!" cried Charlotte, opening the door wide. "Do come in!"

"Is it bad?" asked Mary eagerly, sounding rather as if she hoped it was.

"Nay, I dinna think so," the man assured her. He stepped inside, apologizing for tracking mud on the floors.

"Don't worry," Charlotte reassured him. "You aren't the first today."

"Sounds like a busy mornin'," the man remarked, following Charlotte into the kitchen. He looked inquiringly around the room, at the stack of plates on the worktable, the full pot of porridge, the panful of sausages growing browner by the minute.

"Oh dear!" Charlotte yelped, snatching the

pan off the coals. "Whew, they aren't burned. That's a mercy."

"Done to a turn, I'd say," said the man. Charlotte bustled him into a chair and sent Mary to fetch some of the clean linen rags Mama kept on hand for bandages. The man watched her, wearing an appreciative grin that made him look more schoolboyish than ever.

"All right, we'd best clean the wound," said Charlotte, reaching for his hand.

"Och, nay, ye needn't bother wi' that," protested the man. "I'll just wrap it up good and tight."

"Oh, no, you must be careful!" cried Charlotte earnestly. "You don't want it to get infected. My brother Lewis had blood poisoning in his finger once, and he almost died."

"Yes, and the finger came *off*!" chimed in Mary, returning to the kitchen with enough linen strips to bandage several dozen cut hands.

"Is that so?" said the man, sounding

somewhat chastened. "Well then, I guess I'd better be a good patient."

He held out the injured hand to Charlotte. She lifted off the blood-soaked handkerchief and saw a jagged scratch on his palm. She dabbed at it with a wet cloth.

"I don't think it's too deep," she murmured. "But perhaps I ought to put some of Mama's burn ointment on it, just to be safe. I know it isn't a burn, but Mama's ointments make everything better."

"Mama?" teased the man in mock surprise. "You mean this isna your house? And me supposin' you were mistress here."

Mary giggled. "No, we have a mama and a papa. They're at the mill helping fish a lady out of the pond."

The man's eyebrows went up in surprise.

"Out of the—" He looked at Charlotte in bewilderment.

"Someone fell in. We don't know who. Mary, hand me one of those bandages!"

"I say, I must beg your pardon," said the

man, while Charlotte daubed the scratch with oinment and wrapped it with one of the clean linen strips. "I've not introduced myself, have I?"

Mary burst into speech. "I'm Mary, and that's Charlotte. The others are all at the pond, except Lewis."

"Och, aye, the pond," said the man. "Well, Miss Mary, Miss Charlotte, 'tis a pleasure to meet you properly at last. My name is—"

"I know!" Mary interrupted. "It's Mack. I heard a man driving a wagon call out to you on the road one day."

"Och, did you now? Aye, that's what they call me, all right. Mack."

"Pleased to meet you, Mr. Mack," said Charlotte shyly.

He laughed again—he certainly did laugh a lot, thought Charlotte.

"Just Mack is fine."

"Oh!" Charlotte was taken aback. The only grown-ups she called by their first names were Will and Lucy, and she had known them most of her life.

"Mack," said Mary, nodding with satisfaction.

Lewis came in from the barn, rubbing his hands together. Charlotte had to fight a smile whenever she looked at her big brother these days, for Lewis was cultivating a set of side whiskers. Lydia had mentioned airily at the dinner table one day that she had heard Miss Emma Dillaway remark that she was a great admirer of side whiskers. A few days later, a red stubble had appeared beside each of Lewis's ears. This had now grown into twin stripes of red whiskers that put Charlotte in mind of hairy ginger-colored caterpillars.

Lewis, absently stroking one of his caterpillars, nodded at Mack and asked Charlotte if there had been any word from the mill.

"None at all," said Charlotte. But just then Tom came clattering in through the lean-to. His round face was flushed red from running.

"It was Mrs. Samuel Gardner," he panted. Then he noticed Mack and blinked in surprise to find a stranger in his house.

Charlotte hastened to introduce them. She could not bring herself to call him just plain Mack; she had to add the "Mister."

"But Mrs. Gardner?" she added.

"She's alive, but only just. Mama's still working over her. We can't make out what happened. There was an awful crowd there. Some folks say she fell in, and some folks say she jumped."

"Jumped!" gasped Charlotte. "But why would—"

A sudden image came to her mind: Mr. Samuel Gardner, leaning against the church with his face twisted in anguish that day in June. It had been the very day Dr. Porter announced that Mr. Gardner was donating a new Bible to the church. Charlotte's mouth fell open. Suppose—suppose Mr. Gardner had donated the Bible because he had been the one who destroyed the original! Suppose he was tormented by his own guilty secret? And Mrs. Gardner had found out, and her shame had driven her to throw herself into the pond?

These thoughts passed through her mind in a flash. She shook her head to chase them away. Lewis was looking at her curiously.

"Say, I'm famished," said Tom. "Are those sausages still hot?"

"As if you'd turn them down even if they weren't," said Charlotte, confusion making her blunt. She could not forget the picture of Mr. Gardner practically crying behind the church. But soon she was too busy playing hostess to think of anything else. She dished out the porridge and sausage and supervised the laying of the parlor table. When she filled a plate for Mack, he protested, but she was firm. Of course he must join them for breakfast.

When they were all gathered around the table, Lewis said the blessing so beautifully that Charlotte nearly burst at the seams with pride. Mack chuckled at Mary and grinned at Charlotte, and he spoke to Lewis as respectfully as if they were the same age, though Mack was a great deal older. He must be as old as Papa, Charlotte guessed, for his hair was going gray at the edges. He had a lively, frank way of speaking that Charlotte liked very much. Yes, he said in answer to Lewis's questions, he had been born in Scotland.

"But I've been an American these twenty years and more," he said. "I've not been back to the auld country since I left when I was not much more than your age."

Mary's eyes grew wide. "But don't you miss your family?"

"Aye, sure I do. I used to write my sister when first I left home," he said, "but then she grew up and got married, and we lost track o' each other."

"Oh, how sad," said Charlotte, without meaning to. Mack winced a little, and she felt sorry. She hadn't meant to make him feel bad.

Mary had no such compunctions. She glared at her brothers. "You'd better not go off and forget to write me," she declared. "I'd . . . I'd be simply *flurious*."

Tom and Lewis burst out laughing.

"No fear, Mary-lass," said Lewis, tousling her hair. "We wouldn't dare forget you."

"We wouldn't want to risk your 'flury,'" teased Tom.

Mack was smiling ruefully. "You put me in mind o' my sister," he told Mary. "She was full o' pluck and spirit, like you."

He went on talking about his sister, telling stories about when they had been young together. Then the mantel clock chimed nine o'clock, and he started to his feet.

"I'd best be going. I've a full day's work ahead o' me at the Point, and I'm expected in Dorchester tomorrow noon." He shook Charlotte's hand with grave politeness. "Thank you kindly for your hospitality, miss. You're a fine nurse, you are!"

## Mack's Story

The clock had ticked off another half hour before Mama and Lydia returned. Lewis had gone ahead to the smithy by then, and Tom had hurried to school, hoping the incident with Mrs. Gardner would excuse his tardiness. Charlotte wondered what Miss Eaton would think when she and Lydia didn't show up. She was supposed to recite a piece in French today. It was a little verse about flowers. At least, Charlotte thought it was about flowers. Truth be told, she understood very few of the words, though

Miss Eaton said her accent was quite good.

Mama sank into a chair and closed her eyes.

"Whew, I'm fair tuckered," she said, smiling a little, for that was a Tucker family joke. But her face grew sober again. "A chancy thing it was. That Mrs. Gardner is lucky to be alive."

"What happened, Mama?" All of Charlotte's pent-up curiosity spilled forth. "Did she really jump in?"

Mama's head shot up. "Who told you that?"

"Tom said he heard some people saying so."

Mama's lips pressed together. "*Some people* ought to mind their own business." She sighed. "The truth is no one kens what happened. But where there's doubt, we must give Mrs. Gardner the benefit o' it. The path is slick there by the pond. Happen she slipped and slid down the bank. 'Tis steep, you ken. Her petticoats took in water like sponges and pulled her right down. Sam Waitt saw her go under, but it took three men to get her out. She'd taken in a deal o' water by then."

Charlotte remembered that Mama and Lydia had not had breakfast. Once more she bustled food onto plates and served them right in their chairs by the fire. Mama waved the food away, saying she was too tired to eat.

"A cup of tea, then?" Charlotte asked.

Mama nodded. Suddenly she spied Mack's handkerchief, which Charlotte had rinsed out and draped over the string Mama used for drying wet dish towels. The bloodstains were fainter but still visible.

"What happened? Mama demanded.

"It's Mack's," said Charlotte and Mary together. They tripped over each other's words, explaining.

"Well, he sounds like a nice man," said Mama, when they had poured out the story. "I'm glad you helped him, Lottie."

Mama decided to keep the girls home that day, in case Mrs. Gardner needed her again later. Charlotte was happy to be working alongside Mama once more, preparing the noon meal. She liked Miss Eaton's, but it was nice to be with Mama, listening to her work-songs.

*Down yonder den there's a plowman lad,*
*And some summer's day he'll be a' my ain.*
*And sing laddie O, and sing laddie aye,*
*The plowman's laddies are a' the go.*

At dinner Lewis talked about Mack again.

"He's been all over the country. Kentucky, Louisiana, Maine. Canada too."

"And Scotland," said Mary. "You mustn't forget Scotland."

"I should think not," teased Papa. "I'll no hear o' anyone in this family forgettin' Scotland!"

"I wish you could have heard Mack's stories, Mama," said Charlotte. "You'd love them. He told us all about when he was a boy. One time he actually sank his sister's only doll on a toy boat, and—"

Mama's pewter mug slipped from her hand,

spilling cider all over her skirt. She seemed not to notice. Her face was starkly pale. The children stared at her in alarm, but Papa's eyes were wide with wonder.

"You dinna think . . ." he said.

"Mama, what is it?" asked Lydia.

"It canna be," Mama croaked. Her hands went to her mouth, and she shook her head. "The name is wrong."

Papa turned to Charlotte. "This Mack fellow, was that his real name? Did he say what his whole name is?"

"No, Papa, he said that's what folks call him because he's a Scot. Tom asked was it short for MacDonald or MacSomething, and he said, 'Nay, but me real name's an English name what doesna match me accent.' He said he'd left home when he was a young man, and he'd been Mack these twenty years."

Again Mama's eyes searched Papa's.

"The doll," she murmured. She looked at Charlotte, and her eyes were piercing. "Did he tell you the name of the doll?"

"Yes," said Charlotte, more puzzled than ever. "Lady Something. Like a noblewoman, you know. Lady—"

"Lady Flora," said Mary.

"Yes, that was it!" Charlotte nodded, but Mama was no longer listening. With a strangled cry she rose to her feet, her chair scraping against the floorboards. Then, to everyone's amazement, she turned and ran out of the house.

## At Gravelly Point

The children stared after her in alarm. "Mama!" cried Mary. "Papa, what's the matter? Where has she gone?"

Papa sat shaking his head, looking dazed. He muttered, "Well, what d'ye know? Great lairds o' thunder!"

"Papa, what is it? What's happening?" asked Charlotte, almost shouting.

Papa gave a start. He too pushed back his chair and rose to his feet. "Come," he said. "Let's go."

"Where?" asked the girls in unison.

Papa grinned. "To Gravelly Point."

Charlotte felt like a firework about to explode. This had been a day of mystery upon mystery, and it was scarcely past noon. She wasn't sure she could take any more surprises.

But the biggest surprise of all was waiting for her at Gravelly Point. When she and her sisters and Lewis, running after Papa, arrived at the end of Tide Mill Lane where the road gave way to the tidal marsh with the skeleton of the Cross Dam taking shape upon it, Charlotte's heart skipped a beat in shock. For there were Mama and Mack with their arms around each other, whirling around in a giddy embrace!

Papa gave a roar and sprang toward them. For a moment Charlotte thought he was going to punch Mack, and she hardly blamed him. But instead Papa clapped Mack on the back, and Mack looked up at him in wonder, and then all three of them, Mama and Papa and Mack, were caught up in that laughing, crying, spinning embrace.

The workmen at Gravelly Point were staring at them as if they were all mad. Charlotte didn't blame *them*, either. She herself was half afraid her parents had gone completely off their heads. Lydia shot her a look of amazement, and Mary was pulling on Lewis's sleeve, shouting, "What is it? What's happening?"

Mack drew back suddenly and looked at Mama and Papa, his eyes filled with tears.

"I canna believe it," he whispered. Then a twinkle came into his eye, and he said, "Well, Martha, I see you still canna keep your frock clean."

Mama looked down at her cider-soaked skirt, and her laugh pealed across the flats. The dam workmen were grinning now, leaning on their pickaxes amid the slabs of puddingstone.

"And you still wi' ink stains on your fingers," replied Mama saucily. "But look at the gray hair o' you!"

Mack looked at Papa, his eyes warm and full of wonder.

"Lew Tucker. When I asked you to look after my sister, I'd no idea you'd take it so seriously."

Papa laughed. "Och, ye've got it wrong, Duncan. It's yer sister looks after me." Charlotte had never heard him speak with such raw emotion choking his voice. He was crying; her big, strong, unflappable papa was crying!

Mary tugged at Charlotte's sleeve.

"I don't understand what they're talking about!" Her high voice rang out above the grown-ups' words. The workmen roared with laughter.

Lewis knelt and put an arm around Mary's shoulder.

"Your Mr. Mack," he said wonderingly, "he must be our uncle. He's Mama's brother!"

Charlotte stared, utterly dumbfounded.

"Then . . ." she murmured, staring at Mack—at her uncle. Duncan, Papa had called him. "Your sister, with the doll . . ."

"Aye," said Uncle Duncan. "'Twas Martha here. Your mother. I wonder she ne'er told you that story herself! Och, but she was angry wi' me!"

"Only just at first," said Mama. "I forgave you."

"After I near about froze my nose off traipsin' across the moor to fetch you the fairy dolls." Uncle Duncan laughed.

"The fairy dolls! I know about those!" cried Charlotte. "But not about Lady Flora. Why didn't you ever tell us about her, Mama?"

"Yes, why?" demanded Mary.

"I . . . I canna rightly say," Mama said. Her voice was soft. "I've not thought o' her these many years."

Papa blew his nose on a rather sooty handkerchief. All of Papa's handkerchiefs were sooty.

"Ye'll come home wi' us, Duncan," he said expectantly. "We've much to catch up on."

"Wild horses couldna keep me away," said Uncle Duncan.

# Heart of Gold

Papa and Lewis did not go back to work that day. Lewis ran to the smithy to tell Will what had happened and just as quickly ran back home. No one wanted to miss a word of what this newly found uncle had to say.

Charlotte was dizzy with the wonder of it. An uncle! She had liked him so much when he was just Mack, the nice surveyor man. Now that he was Uncle Duncan, she felt shy. But she crowded close to him in the parlor with the others, unable to tear her eyes off him lest he should disappear like a wraith in one of Mama's stories.

Uncle Duncan was no wraith. He was hearty and solid and real. He laughed like Mama, with his eyes crinkled into half-moons. He peppered Mama with questions, and she peppered him right back. They were each so eager to hear about the other that they scarcely paused to answer, until Papa, laughing, held up his hands and told Uncle Duncan he'd better go first.

Uncle Duncan had left Scotland when he was a young man about Lewis's age. He had sailed to Canada and "knocked around awhile," as he put it, in the north. When he needed money, he went to the nearest town and painted portraits of wealthy people. Governors especially, said Uncle Duncan, were always glad to have their wives' portraits taken. Uncle Duncan had painted pictures of three governors' wives.

"But it's chancy work, paintin'," he continued. "No guarantee you'll find work when

you need it. I took up mapmakin' to buy me
bread between portraits. Plenty o' work for
a man who's a steady hand at inkin'. After a
while that led me to surveyin'. I fell in wi'
Mr. Hales, oh, three years ago it was. I've
been to every hamlet in two counties, doin'
survey work for Hales's new map."

"I canna believe," Mama said, "you've been
here for weeks and us nivver kennin' it!"

Uncle Duncan shook his head ruefully.
"More's the pity. I'm about finished here. I'm
off to Dorchester tomorrow afternoon."

Papa looked disappointed. "And me hopin'
ye'd stay on a bit wi' us."

"I'd like naught better," Uncle Duncan
said, "but I've given my word to Hales."

"Canna be helped then," said Papa. "But
Dorchester's none too far. Ye'll come back
and visit us, aye?"

"I should think he will! Every Sunday, at
the very least," declared Mama. "Now leave
off talkin' as if he's steppin' out the door this
minute. Ye're bidin' here tonight, Duncan,
and I'll no hear a word to the contrary. We'll

send you off to Dorchester wi' a full belly in the mornin'."

"All right," laughed Uncle Duncan. "I'd not dare to argue wi' you, Martha. I'll have to go back to the Point for a while, though. I've a last sightin' to take down there."

"Can I come?" pleaded Mary. Charlotte hoped for an invitation too. But Mama said they'd be sure to slow him down, and she didn't want to be robbed of a single minute with her brother.

"You go on and do your work, but mind you hurry back," she ordered. "We'll have us a feast for supper tonight. But first we'll have to clean up from dinner," she added, with a wry glance at the forgotten meal on the table, and a pool of sticky cider drying on the floor by her chair.

Papa said he might as well go back to the shop after all. Lewis went with him. Charlotte and Lydia helped Mama all afternoon, cooking and cleaning. Mama killed a chicken and fricasseed it, using a whole cupful of butter in the gravy. Mary wandered in and out of the kitchen, sniffing loudly and holding her stomach to show how hungry she was. Mama passed out doughnuts to tide everyone over. No one had eaten much dinner that day.

It seemed as though Uncle Duncan would never return, but at last he tapped on the lean-to door, a battered satchel in his hand.

"I went to the boardinghouse for my things," he explained.

No one wanted to go to bed that night. There were too many stories to hear, questions to ask. Mama and Papa and Uncle Duncan (whom Mary could not seem to call anything but Mack) told about their growing-up days in Scotland. Papa and Uncle Duncan had gone to school together when they were very young. When they were Charlotte's age, Uncle Duncan had been sent away to a very fine school in Perth, and Papa had stopped going to school altogether. He had stayed with his father to learn his trade.

"Were you sent away to school too?" Charlotte asked Mama.

"Aye, but not until later. I was home a good

many years after Duncan went to school. Saw more of your father in those years, I did, than my own brothers."

Papa grinned. "A wild, free lass yer mother was, always flittin' across the grass wi' that red hair streamin' back. Us lads in the village used to jump at any chance to run errands for our fathers on her side o' the loch. Not a one of us ivver dreamt o' marryin' her, though."

Color rushed up into Mama's cheeks, and her eyes sparkled.

"You ought to have dreamed o' it, Lew Tucker," she said boldly. "I did, when I came back from school."

"Didn't you ever dream of marrying someone, Uncle Duncan?" asked Lydia, leaning eagerly forward, her hands clasped. She loved stories about people falling in love. Charlotte noticed that Lewis, too, was listening with interest. She smiled to herself, delighting in her secret knowledge. It was exciting to have a brother old enough to be courting someone.

Uncle Duncan looked thoughtful.

"Nay, I canna say that I did. I've always had

such an itch to roam the country. Wives dinna take too well to that sort o' life."

Mama snorted. "Some might. You ought to ask someone and find out. Besides, when the bairns started comin', you might find you didna have such a hankerin' to wander. Children have a way o' makin' you glad to be where you can put down roots."

Uncle Duncan glanced round at them all: Papa leaning back in his chair with Mary on his knee, Mama with her cap strings dangling and her knitting lying ignored in her lap, Lewis and Tom and Lydia and Charlotte clustered around them.

"Aye," he said softly, "I can see they might at that."

It was a sorrowful parting the next morning. Mama was up before daylight, cooking, determined to send her brother off with another feast. But no one ate much breakfast. Charlotte fought a lump in her throat. She hated to think of Uncle Duncan leaving. Now that they had found him, she wanted to keep him forever.

He promised to write from Dorchester. Papa kept reminding everyone that Dorchester was only a few miles away. Uncle Duncan could come for Sunday dinner as often as he liked.

He hugged them each in turn, starting and finishing with Mama. He said nothing in the world could have made him so happy as knowing how happy she was.

"A finer family," he said, "I've yet to see in all my travels."

After he had gone, Charlotte noticed a parcel on the dinner table, in front of Mama's seat. It was a lumpy package of brown paper tied with string.

"What on earth?" said Mama. "Duncan must have left it, bless him!"

"It's a present! Open it!" cried Mary.

The whole family crowded around to watch Mama open it. As the paper wrappings fell away, Mama drew in a trembling breath, her hand to her mouth. She picked up the gift and stared at it wonderingly.

"'Tis a doll!" said Lydia. It was a slender

wooden doll with a painted face, of the kind Charlotte had seen in Bacon's General Store. She had painted hair and was clothed in a dress made of green linen. Mama closed her eyes, swallowing back tears. She pressed her lips to the doll's smooth brown hair.

"That scoundrel," she murmured. Papa put his arm around her shoulder.

"That's why he took so long coming back yesterday, I'll bet," said Tom.

"Is it Lady Flora, Mama?" asked Mary, crinkling her forehead. "I thought she was lost."

Mama smiled. "She was. This dolly is very like her. My brother has a heart o' gold, he does."

"Will you name this one Lady Flora too?" asked Charlotte.

"May I play with her?" begged Mary.

Mama's golden laugh rang out.

"Aye, but I'm warnin' you right now. You're to keep her away from the water!"

# *George*

After that, Uncle Duncan came from Dorchester every week to spend the day with the Tuckers. He went to Sunday meeting with them and came home with them for dinner. And what dinners they were! Mama spent all day Saturday baking. When Charlotte and Lydia came home from school on Saturday afternoons, the pantry shelf was lined with pies. Meat pies, berry pies, raisin pies, pear pies. At Sunday dinner Uncle Duncan would shake his head in wonder over those pies.

"Cook would be proud," he'd say. "I've not tasted fare like this since I left home."

"Dear Cook," Mama murmured. "I still canna match her jam. Och, the taste o' her bilberry preserves on a warm bannock!"

"Canna be as good as your pear pie, Martha!" said Uncle Duncan emphatically.

At harvesttime Uncle Duncan had to leave. His work in Dorchester was finished, and Mr. Hales was sending him up the coast. He would be too far away to come back on Sundays. Everyone in the family was dismayed.

"But after that, 'tis back to Boston," said Uncle Duncan. "I'm to help Hales combine the surveys. I should have quite a long stay there, I imagine."

That cheered them up. Boston was even closer than Dorchester.

"You could board wi' us," Mama pointed out. "'Tis no such a long walk over the Neck and back."

"Aye, and when that dam road opens, 'twill be a shorter walk still," said Papa.

Uncle Duncan laughed.

"We'll see. Ye'll have more than enough work on your hands already, wi'out wearin' yourself out makin' six kinds o' pie for the likes o' me."

He was referring, Charlotte knew, to the impending arrival of the baby. It would not be long now. Mama's belly was too big to be hidden by a loose gown. It was very large and round now. Sometimes, when she sat down in her favorite chair in the parlor, she could not get back up without help.

One night in late October, just as the term at Miss Eaton's was drawing to a close, Charlotte woke well before sunup. She heard a commotion of footsteps and voices in the kitchen below and thought she had gotten up and gone down to see what the matter was when suddenly she woke up and found it was morning. Dimly she recalled the sounds of distant bustle in the dark. Now in the golden dawn, the house was hushed, sleeping—and then she heard a thin cry, and she knew the baby had arrived.

It was a boy. He was named George, after Papa's father. The very day he was born, Charlotte added his name to her family record sampler.

## George Drummond Tucker born

## Oct 20th 1820

She had forgotten how small a newborn baby could be. When she held him, he was lighter than a goose-feather pillow. She had held newborn babies before, but never one who belonged to her. She had been too little at Mary's birth.

The midwife told Papa to make sure Mama got plenty of rest.

"I know her sort," the old woman said, waggling a gnarled finger. "She's apt to think the house'll fall down around her ears if she's not up on her feet a-running all day. Don't you let her do it. Let these daughters of yours take care of things. I'll warrant they're more than capable. You mark my words, now."

Papa marked them. He sent word to Miss Eaton that the girls would have to miss the end of the term. He arranged for them to take their exams later, after Mama was back on her feet. A week earlier Charlotte would have been dismayed to think of missing those last few days in the sweet-scented parlor, agonizing with Ellie over French verbs and principal rivers, and admiring the other girls' finished velvet landscapes (which, she had to admit, were every bit as blurry as Mama had predicted). Now Miss Eaton's school seemed a thousand miles away.

It seemed to Charlotte that her life had been divided into two neat parts: *before George* and *after George*. *After George* was busier, noisier, and indescribably sweeter. The sisters fought over whose turn it was to hold him. At first they fought over whose turn it was to change him, too, but the novelty of that task quickly faded. And there was never any squabbling at all over who would wash out his soiled clouts. Mary flatly refused, and

Charlotte and Lydia took turns, keeping careful track of whose turn it was.

Charlotte expected Mama to fuss about being waited on, but instead she seemed happy to sit and rest, cradling the baby in her arms, while the girls bustled about doing the housework. *Now* she would let Charlotte serve her. Her eyes twinkled with mirth when Charlotte brought her a cup of tea or tucked a shawl around her shoulders, and she played along, nodding graciously and thanking Charlotte in uppity accents.

Charlotte had been making doll clothes for years, and she found herself on delightfully comfortable ground when it came to making garments for the baby. Lydia found sewing tedious, so she volunteered to knit for George, producing an array of tiny booties and caps that sent Mary into a swoon of delight. Tom rolled his eyes and pretended to be disgusted with the girls' raptures over all things George, but Charlotte wasn't fooled. Tom did his share of fighting for a turn to hold the baby. They all spoiled him, from Papa and

Lewis right on down.

One Sunday Uncle Duncan came all the way from Salem to see the baby. He could stay only two hours, and he spent nearly the whole time leaning back in a chair with George nestled on his chest and his feet propped before the fire.

"Looks like Alisdair, he does," he told Mama. Charlotte knew that was another uncle, Mama's oldest brother. She loved to hear Mama and Uncle Duncan talk about the people they had left behind: their parents, their two brothers, their sister, Grisie, Grisie's children, Mama's cousins, Papa's brothers— there were so many people, a whole crowd of family Charlotte had never met. She hadn't known some of them existed until now. Yet it was obvious Mama loved them and missed them. Charlotte tried to imagine herself grown up, living far away from Mama and Papa, never seeing them, not even knowing if they were still alive. It was impossible to imagine.

Now that she knew about this host of

cousins and aunts and uncles, she missed them too. She did not know what they looked like nor even what all their names were—-Mama and Uncle Duncan's stories had come so fast and thick, it was hard to keep them all straight—but Charlotte missed them all the same. When she looked at baby George, she thought of Uncle Alisdair and wondered if she would ever see him.

November came. Charlotte and Lydia went to Miss Eaton's for a day to take their exams in French, geography, and English composition. Neither one of them had studied. Charlotte knew she had completely mixed up her principal rivers of Europe, but she thought her composition was all right. French was anyone's guess. Lydia said she was sure she had failed them all. Miss Eaton smiled her prim smile and said, "We'll see."

Her mother took them into the sitting room for a plate of cookies while Miss Eaton marked their papers. She asked about the baby, and Charlotte told her eagerly how bright and hearty he was.

"He looks right into my eyes as if he knows me already," she said proudly. Mrs. Eaton isn't-that-lovely'd politely, but Charlotte could see she was not really as impressed as she pretended to be. And when Miss Eaton came in shortly thereafter to tell the girls they had both passed in all subjects, and Charlotte had made very high marks in composition and geography, Charlotte found herself making the same kind of falsely enthusiastic responses to her teacher as old Mrs. Eaton had made to her about George's brilliance. She would never want to hurt Miss Eaton's feelings by saying so, but how on earth could French verbs and foreign cities compare to a baby whose big searching eyes looked right into hers as if there were nothing in the world he would rather see?

# Auntie Rho

The day after George's first smile, the first snowfall came to Roxbury. It was met with cheers of delight from the whole family. During the brutal heat of summer Charlotte had longed for snow, dreamed of throwing herself into snowdrifts and lying there reveling in blessed cold. She was eager to get outside and play in it, but she had to wait until the next day when the blizzard finally wore itself out.

Mama said she had never seen so much snow in her life. The road was completely covered; no wagons would disturb the peace that day. From the dooryard there extended a field of snow unbroken save for the birch thicket as far as Charlotte could see. Across the glittering fields a curl of smoke smudged the pale sky: That was Farmer Heath's house, half a mile away.

At first there was nothing to see but what they could see from the windows. No one could get out of the house. When Charlotte opened the lean-to door, she was met by a perfect wall of snow as high as her knees. She thought its clean, level edge was one of the most beautiful things she had ever seen. No human mason could build a wall that straight and smooth. Then Mary barreled past her and sank both hands into the snow. The perfect wall crumbled onto Charlotte's boots. Mary ate a mouthful of snow and then dropped the rest on the floor, exclaiming over the cold. Mama told Charlotte to shut the door before the drift caved in upon the floor.

After that no one could bear to be indoors, except Mama, who had to stay with the baby, of course. Tom and Lewis had brought their sleds in from the back shed when the first flakes began to fall, to have them polished and ready the moment the storm was over. Lewis prepared for sledding with all the eagerness of a young boy. Forgotten, for the moment, were his side whiskers and his sober grown-up dignity. Miss Emma Dillaway was safely across town beyond drifted, unbroken roads, anyway, unable to witness his wild, whooping descents down Great Hill with the youngsters.

It snowed again the following week. Then it snowed three times in one week, one blizzard blowing into the next. By the middle of December Charlotte no longer felt as affectionate toward snow as she had at first. Each storm undid Papa and the boys' efforts to clear paths between house and barn and smithy. Charlotte dreaded the shivering walk to the outhouse—when, indeed, the walk could be attempted. She held a private opinion that the emptying of chamber pots was a task for which Mama would cheerfully accept one of Lady Rowena's servants.

Around Christmas there was a stretch of clear days. Roxbury folk gathered gladly at the church, hungry for fellowship after so many days of isolation. Some men started a petition to raise money for an organ. The notion met with with great enthusiasm— properly sober, of course, in consideration of the sacred surroundings. Someone suggested that Miss Emma Dillaway could be engaged to play for church services. Miss Emma blushed until she matched her pink bonnet strings, and Lewis grinned with pride.

The next week Mama sent Charlotte and Lydia to Bacon's General Store to buy some lump sugar and nutmeg. Outside the shop they ran into Ellie Till's mother. She greeted them warmly and invited them to stop at her house for a cup of cider on their way home.

"Ellie will be glad to see you, Charlotte," she said. Charlotte's heart leaped at the prospect. She had scarcely seen Ellie at all this winter. But she knew Mama was waiting for the nutmeg. And it was beginning to snow again.

"I'd love to, ma'am, but I guess we'd better

get home," she said reluctantly.

Lydia shrugged and reached for the parcel Charlotte was carrying.

"Why don't you go ahead, Lottie? I'll tell Mama. She won't mind."

"That's all right, then," said Ellie's mother. "I'll send her along home shortly." Lydia went one direction, cutting across the common toward home, and Charlotte followed Mrs. Till down Washington Street toward the funny old house in which Ellie lived.

Ellie was thrilled to see her. Her younger sisters, Abigail and Catherine, came running to see what the excitement was about. Little Catherine clutched Abigail's hand, staring at Charlotte with shy, admiring eyes. Charlotte felt pleasantly mature and sophisticated, though Catherine was not much younger than Mary. Charlotte supposed she and Ellie, going on twelve, must seem quite grown up to a five-year-old.

"I know a secret," Catherine announced solemnly. "It's about Aunt Ruth."

Aunt Ruth lived in the other wing of the

large Till house, with her brother, Ellie's
Uncle Asa. Ellie's elderly great-aunt Rhoda
Jane lived there too. She was bedridden and
frail, but she had a lively tongue and a sharp
wit. Charlotte had visited her many times.
Auntie Rho liked to have young people
around her, she said.

Ellie's grandfather had lived in the Uncle
Asa wing, too, but he had died last winter.
Grandfather Jonas had been Auntie Rho's
brother, and Ellie said her mother had worried that all the snap would go out of Auntie
Rho when she didn't have Grandfather to
fight with. But Auntie Rho seemed plenty
snappy to Charlotte.

Ellie was pouncing on Catherine.

"What kind of secret?" she demanded.
"Are you allowed to tell?"

"No, she isn't," said Ellie's mother. "But if
you run up to see Aunt Ruth, she'll tell you
herself."

Locking hands, Charlotte and Ellie ran to
the door that connected to the Uncle Asa side
of the house. At the threshold they stopped

running, because Uncle Asa didn't allow it. He was gruff and stern. Walking on the balls of their feet, they crept to the stairs and hurried up them. It was impossible to hurry and creep at the same time. They heard Uncle Asa growling from the room below, but by then they were safely in Aunt Ruth's chamber. She was a weaver, and she worked at her loom all day.

"Ma says you have news!" burst out Ellie, without saying hello.

Aunt Ruth's sober gray eyes had a twinkle in them today. She was a quiet, busy woman, not given to much twinkling. But she was certainly twinkling today.

In her brisk, matter-of-fact way, she answered, "Yes. I'm getting married in the spring."

Charlotte clapped her hands. She always liked to hear about weddings. Ellie was thunderstruck. Aunt Ruth laughed at the frank amazement on Ellie's face.

"Who?" asked Ellie. "Who are you marrying?"

"Whom," said Aunt Ruth. "Titus Faxon. I'm surprised you haven't guessed already, Elizabeth. He has come calling every week for months."

Ellie opened and closed her mouth like a fish.

"To see Uncle Asa, I thought," she said. "They're friends. Aren't they? Mr. Faxon seems so—so old!"

Aunt Ruth smiled placidly. "Well, as far as that goes, I'm not such a young woman myself. Mr. Faxon is a fine man. He'll make you a fine uncle. You'll see."

Charlotte understood a little of Ellie's amazement. Aunt Ruth was the last person she would have guessed would be getting married. She was so quiet and serious. She did not seem interested in anything except her work.

Charlotte and Ellie discussed the astonishing news all the way back to Ellie's side of the house. They agreed that they would rather be old maids than marry a gray-whiskered old man like Mr. Titus Faxon.

"Auntie Rho's an old maid," said Ellie. "She seems cheerful enough."

When they got back to Ellie's parlor, her mother was looking anxiously out the window. The snow was falling heavily now. It looked like the beginnings of a blizzard.

"You'll have to stay here, Charlotte," she said. "I dare not send you home in such a storm as this."

"But they'll be worried at home," Charlotte fretted. "Mama will think I got lost in the storm. Suppose Papa goes out looking for me, and gets lost, and freezes! Suppose—"

"Hush, child," said Mrs. Till. "Don't get yourself excited. Lydia knows you came here, don't she? Your mother will reckon you had the good sense to stay put. Anyway, it doesn't matter whether she worries or not—I can't send you out in this weather, and that's that."

Charlotte opened her mouth and closed it again. She wished she were more like Mama. Mama wouldn't let anyone make her stay when she wanted to go. She'd just up and go. Charlotte couldn't do it, couldn't defy

Mrs. Till. It wouldn't be good manners, and worse than that, it might be a sin. Charlotte couldn't be sure; it seemed wrong to put Mama and the others through the anguish of worry, and perhaps to put Papa's life at risk. But she supposed Papa was more likely to manage a two-mile walk in blinding snow than she was. She would have to mind Mrs. Till.

Ellie was delighted, and she at once whisked Charlotte up to her bedchamber to pick out a nightgown for that evening. Ellie had two, and she offered Charlotte her choice.

"The woolen is warmer, but it itches," said Ellie. "The flannel is softer. I put those sleeves in myself," she added proudly.

Abigail hurried into the room. "Auntie Rho wants you, Charlotte. She says it's your turn to entertain her."

"Entertain her?" gasped Charlotte. "I wouldn't know how!"

Ellie laughed. "Oh, that just means she wants you to read to her. Or tell her a story."

"Tell her a story!"

"I shouldn't think it would be too hard for you. Your family is such a one for telling stories."

Charlotte followed Ellie back to Uncle Asa's side of the house, wondering what story to tell. She liked Auntie Rho a great deal, but the old woman had a way of coming at you with surprises. This was a new one.

"Aha," said Auntie Rho, propped up on pillows in her bed, which stood prominently in the parlor, hung with a canopy of curtains.

Auntie Rho had a sharp voice that sounded cross but never was. She was a tiny, bright-eyed old woman, with a wrinkled face and a long braid of hair draped over her shoulder. The braid was tied with a red hair ribbon, just like a little girl's.

"There you are. I saw you go creepin' past before. Too high and mighty to spare a few minutes on a poor invalid, eh?"

Aghast, Charlotte opened her mouth to protest, and Auntie Rho cackled with laughter. She liked to tease.

"Go ahead, sit down," she said, patting the

bed. Obligingly Charlotte climbed up to sit beside the old woman, dangling her legs off the edge. Ellie found a spot at the foot of the bed.

"Let's have a story," ordered Auntie Rho. "A good one."

The only thing that came into Charlotte's head was *Ivanhoe*. She decided that would do nicely. Auntie Rho couldn't ask for a more exciting story than that. She dived in and was just telling of the moment in which the sinister Norman knight, Sir Brian de Bois-Guilbert, first laid greedy eyes upon the proud and beautiful Lady Rowena, when Mrs. Till entered Auntie Rho's parlor to tell the girls supper would be ready soon.

"Suppertime my eye!" snapped Auntie Rho. "I want to hear the end of this story."

"I'm sorry, Auntie, it must wait. Perhaps Charlotte can tell some more tomorrow before she goes home."

"Humph. Maybe I'll get lucky and it'll keep on snowing for a week, like it did when I was a girl. Jonas and I were tending the

stock when the blizzard hit, and we couldn't
see to get back to the house. We burrowed
into the hay to keep from freezing, and we
lived on turnips and raw grain for three days
until Papa dug us out. Mama thought we'd
lost our way in the storm and frozen to death.
The worry nearly killed her."

Charlotte swallowed hard.

"Don't fret, child," said Mrs. Till quickly.
"I'm sure your mother isn't worried." She cast
a stern glance at Auntie Rho.

The old woman snorted again. "Humph.
Well, mind you come see me in the morning,
Charlotte, and finish this story."

"Yes, ma'am," said Charlotte. "Only—it's a
very long story. I've only just gotten started,
really."

"What do you mean? What did you go and
start it for, if it's too long to finish in a sitting?
Or two sittings, even! You've got me all
worked up now. I won't rest till I know how it
ends."

"I'm sorry," gasped Charlotte.

Auntie Rho looked at her with glittering

eyes. "You ought to be. I'll tell you what. You'll just have to come back here and tell it to me until it's finished. I don't have forever, mind. Don't you let any old snowstorms keep you away. Otherwise we may just have to keep you here until you finish."

She lay back on her pillow, nodding at the canopy.

"That ought to carry me through the winter, at any rate. I'm determined to live long enough to see Ruth married."

Now it was Ellie's turn to gasp.

"Auntie! You aren't . . ." Her voice trailed off into a question.

"Dying? Course I am! Eventually. I'm eighty-one years old. There ain't ten people in this town older'n me. That heat last summer took the stuffing out of me. I can't hardly hold a teacup anymore long enough to get a sip. Ain't you got eyes in your head, girl?"

The old lady delivered this surprising speech without the least bit of anger or worry in her voice. Indeed, she grinned at the girls

as impishly as ever. Charlotte didn't know
what to say. She had the idea she ought to say
reassuring things about how of course Auntie
Rho wasn't going to die anytime soon, but she
sensed the words would be empty.

Ellie, too, was at a loss for words.

"Auntie Rho," she quavered, trailing off.

"My gracious," said Auntie Rho. "Look at
the long faces. I ain't planning to go *tonight*,
you know." She chuckled. "Course it ain't
really up to me, is it? I reckon the Almighty
can manage the details o' my comings and
goings without a lot of fuss from me. Not but
what I'd like to have a little say in it, mind
you."

She looked upward again, but this time her
sharp eyes stared up through the canopy, past
it. "You know, Lord, that I'd dearly like to see
our Ruthie come down those stairs in a silk
gown. I suppose it'd be a bit much to ask to
see Miss Elizabeth here on her wedding day.
Though she'll make a prettier bride than
Ruthie and me put together, won't she? You
outdone yourself with her, Lord, and I don't

stick at saying so even if she is Jonas's grand-
child instead of my own. Amen."

She turned her wrinkled face back toward
the girls, adding, "I'm not saying your Aunt
Ruth isn't handsome, mind. She's not what
you'd call beautiful, but she's got a snap to
her you don't see in many young folk nowa-
days. Asa's always worried she'd die an old
maid like me."

Charlotte thought of a question and
decided she would ask it. Surely a person who
spoke as frankly as Auntie Rho wasn't likely
to mind frankness in others. Quickly, before
she lost her nerve, she tumbled out the question.

"Do you mind being an old maid, Auntie?"

The piercing black eyes fixed upon hers.
Auntie Rho smiled, a slow, thoughtful smile
unlike her usual mocking grin.

"Well now, ain't that a treat. A person with
some sense. All these years I been listening to
folks cluck their tongues over my 'sad and
lonely' state. Ain't a one of them ever asked
me if I minded it."

She reached out her thin arms, small in the sleeves of her faded linen gown, and took hold of Charlotte's hands. Her fingers were knobby, the skin loose and cold. But she gave Charlotte's hands a squeeze of surprising strength—one quick squeeze, as if that were all the exertion she could manage.

"No, child, I don't mind. Here's how I figure it. God could have given me more, but He could have given me a good deal less. I've always had plenty o' family around me; plenty for me to help look after when I was spry, and plenty to look after me now I ain't. I've had a roof over my head most every night of my life, and a meal in my belly most every day. That's a good deal to be happy about. I never had no husband to cosset me—nor fuss at me neither. I reckon marriage is like most other things, got its ups and downs. My life's been more steady like. I ain't the kind o' person who turns up her nose at what's served her, just 'cause it ain't something else. I ate what the Almighty served me, and it filled me up just fine."

She squeezed Charlotte's hand again.

"Eat what you're served, child, and season it any way you like. You do that and you'll get along all right."

# The Truth about Mr. Gardner

**P**apa came for Charlotte late the following afternoon, after the roads were broken. He bundled her into Mr. Waitt's sleigh, tucking her under several layers of heavy woolen rugs. He said Mama hadn't worried much; she trusted Charlotte to have the good sense to stay at Ellie's.

"We missed you, though," he added, his eyes smiling at her above his red muffler.

"Did George miss me?" Charlotte asked,

feeling a pang at having missed a whole day of his life.

"Aye, that he did. And I hear Mary hardly slept a wink wi'out her Lottie to kick under the covers."

The rest of the winter was so busy and full, Charlotte felt breathless keeping up with it. Whenever the weather and Mama permitted, she walked to Ellie Till's to tell a little more of *Ivanhoe* to Auntie Rho. Charlotte read the book on her own at home to be sure not to miss one thrilling detail. Ellie and her sisters listened eagerly also, and often gruff Uncle Asa found a reason to sit in Auntie Rho's parlor when Charlotte was in the middle of an episode. Ivanhoe's adventures seemed to paint the dull white days of winter with vibrant color: the red crosses, the purple silks, the green forests, the gleaming golden crowns.

At home there were adventures of a different sort. They were not so grand in scale as sword fights in English forests, but they were in their own way just as exciting to Charlotte.

Every week seemed to mark some marvelous new accomplishment for baby George. He rolled over. He laughed. He sat up by himself for a whole seven seconds. He shook a silver rattle without any help. He pulled hair. He babbled. He cut a tooth and cried all night. He learned to crawl. He crawled halfway up the stairs and fell back down, giving Mama a terrible fright.

By April he had to be watched every minute lest he should scoot his way into the fire or some other peril. Lucy Payson gave birth to another little girl. Compared to tiny Josephine, George looked enormous. He was stocky and sturdy as a calf. And smart as a whip, Mama declared. He had a way of looking right into a person's eyes and uttering a stream of sounds, just as if he were talking. Charlotte was convinced he *was* saying words, if she could only understand them. Mama said he was too young to be talking for real, but Charlotte believed George capable of any achievement. He was the cleverest, heartiest, handsomest baby in the whole world.

The ladies of the neighborhood seemed to agree. Lucy admired his strong grasp and his two fine teeth. Mrs. Porter said his chin was remarkably like George Washington's. Mrs. Samuel Waitt said she had never seen a prettier baby, even if he did have red hair. Mama gritted her teeth at that but let it go. Later, at supper, she told Papa, and he teased her about it for weeks.

"Ah, me, that was a fine meal," he would say, patting his belly. "Ye're quite a cook, Mrs. Tucker, even if ye do have red hair."

Mama repaid him with the saucy words she was too polite to use on Mrs. Waitt. Mrs. Waitt, she maintained, was a kind soul and a good friend, even if she had no more tact than a rooster.

Mrs. Waitt came to visit often that spring, toting her sewing along in a basket. She was full of complaints about the Mill Dam. Already Mr. Waitt was suffering from its effects. The water level in the flats was dropping. Stony Brook, which fed Mrs. Waitt's gristmill, was drying up. The mill pond was becoming a puddle.

"Letitia Gardner could throw herself into it now and be none the worse." Mrs. Waitt sighed.

"Whisht," Mama scolded, looking stern over her spinning wheel. "She says she slipped and fell. Not havin' been there myself, I'm inclined to give her the benefit o' the doubt."

She glanced significantly at Charlotte and Mary, who were playing a game of checkers in the corner. (For the most part the game consisted of removing checkers from George's fists before he could cram them into his mouth.)

"Humph. You're a charitable soul, Martha. I have my private opinions about what happened that day, and I don't mind saying so. Letitia Gardner has never been in her right mind since their girl died." Mrs. Waitt sighed mournfully. "Dear me, what a vale of tears this life is. Of course the child was never strong, you know. A weak heart, I believe. Such a sweet girl, and only six years old. Just like your Mary."

143

Mama's spinning wheel hummed with unusual force.

"Mary is seven now," she said, as if placing her firmly in a category of children unlikely to be afflicted by weak hearts.

Charlotte had been listening intently. She blurted out a question without thinking.

"Is that why Mr. Gardner was crying behind the church last summer?"

Both Mama and Mrs. Waitt stared at her.

She flushed. "I mean, I don't know if he was crying exactly. He was sad. I saw him . . . he was covering his face with his hands. It was the day they announced he was giving the new Bible."

Mrs. Waitt cut a sharp glance at Mama.

"Now isn't that curious . . ." she said. It sounded as if she were thinking a great deal more.

Mama whisked the subject on to other things. Emma Dillaway was doing a lovely job as organist, wasn't she? What a treat it was to have real music at Sunday meeting. That led to a torrent of lively questions from Mrs.

Waitt about whether she was correct in supposing that young Lewis was a trifle sweet on Miss Dillaway, and wouldn't she make a fine wife?

But after Mrs. Waitt left, Mama pulled Charlotte aside.

"I want to talk to you about Mr. and Mrs. Gardner."

Charlotte winced. "I'm sorry, Mama. I didn't mean to tell secrets. I didn't tell all this time, but it just slipped out."

"I'd like to know," said Mama slowly, "why you feel it was a secret, your seeing Mr. Gardner like that."

"Well . . ." Charlotte tried to sort it out. It wasn't something she had thought; it was something she had felt, or sensed.

"It seemed so . . . private. A big man like that, almost crying. It was like he was in pain."

She bit her lip, looking into Mama's clear eyes.

"Mama," she said, almost whispering, "the way it happened right after Dr. Porter said

Mr. Gardner was donating the new Bible. I thought . . . I thought maybe he was the one who ripped up the old one. And everyone blamed it on drunken quarrymen, but really it was Mr. Gardner, and then he felt so guilty he bought a new one."

"Why, Charlotte Tucker," said Mama, and Charlotte quailed, knowing she was in for a scolding. It was a sin to bear false witness against a neighbor; she knew that. Did it count as "bearing false witness" if you only made a guess about something? She had not said it was definitely true.

But Mama surprised her.

"You're a perceptive lass, you are. I never saw the like o' you for watchin', and noticin', and puttin' two and two together."

"What?" Charlotte gasped. "You mean I'm right?"

"I didna say that. You're not far off, though. And you kept your own counsel about it all this time. I'm proud o' you for that, lass, for it *was* a private moment you saw, and it would indeed have been wrong o' you to spread

146

rumors about a thing when you didna ken all the facts. Since you held your tongue so well, I dinna mind tellin' you the truth o' the matter. You're to hold your tongue about this as well, you understand."

"Yes, Mama," gulped Charlotte, feeling very grown-up. Mama was going to confide in her. Mama thought she was perceptive!

"After Mrs. Gardner fell into the pond last summer," Mama said, "and I helped save her life, she came to me to talk. Poured out her heart, she did, and I never expected to tell another soul. But I'm tellin' you."

Her voice was low and calm. "It wasna Mr. Gardner who destroyed the old Bible. 'Twas *Mrs.* Gardner."

"Mama!" Charlotte's voice was shrill in her surprise.

"Aye, it's true. She had lost her wee daughter, as you heard Mrs. Waitt say. I dinna think you knew Helen; she was never strong enough to go to school. She was a frail wee thing. Slipped away early last spring, she did. Mrs. Waitt was correct in guessin' that grief put Mrs. Gardner out o' her right mind for a time. Mad at God, she was, the poor woman. The sorrow turned to anger and, aye, even hatred in her heart, and she lost hold o' her senses. She went into the church, and she tore up that Bible and took a knife to the cushions in the pulpit. And then, when she realized what she had done, she hated her own self."

Charlotte found herself twisting her apron in her hands. She felt caught up between pity and horror. Poor Mrs. Gardner, being out of her mind with grief! But to think of doing what she had done!

Mama went on. "I reckon her husband figured out what happened. Perhaps she told him; I dinna ken. But he did the right thing and replaced the Bible, even though it must have been a bitter pill for the both o' them to face the gratitude and praise o' the church. I daresay he asked Dr. Porter to keep his identity a secret, but the Reverend is such a magnanimous sort, he canna bear to see anyone robbed o' credit they're owed. So he announced it at meeting, and what you saw afterward was Mr. Gardner sufferin' from those terrible coals o' fire that had been heaped on his head."

"Mama," Charlotte said, almost whispering, "did Mrs. Gardner really throw herself into the pond?"

Mama's eyes were grave. "Aye, she did, Charlotte. And make no mistake about it, that was a worse thing than what she did in the church. The one was an act born of grief; the other was an act of despair. We must never give in to despair, never. It's a mercy she survived. She's made her peace wi' God, now, and her broken heart will heal."

As if to lift the heavy mood, Mama reached out and tugged one of Charlotte's brown curls.

"That's between you, me, and the wall, you hear?"

Charlotte found herself looking at the wall as if it could spill the secret. She felt almost giddy with relief. She wasn't even sure what she was relieved about. She was glad Mrs.

Gardner was alive and back in her right mind. She was glad to know Mr. Gardner wasn't a secret criminal.

And underneath the lifted weight of those dark worries, there was something else, something new and pleasant. She was savoring Mama's praise and trust. Mama had shared a secret with her that she had not shared with anyone else, not Lydia, or Mrs. Waitt, or even Papa. She felt a thrill of closeness to her mother. She realized with a jolt that she was not a little girl anymore. She would be twelve soon; she was growing up.

# Papa's News

With the advent of spring, construction of the dams had resumed at a heightened pace. The Mill Dam was all but complete, and the Cross Dam was coming along fast. The Mill Dam Corporation was eager to see the job finished. Already Boston businessmen were filing requests to open stores and mills along the new dam roads. The flats were drying up, just as Mama had predicted. The big Mill Dam walled off the water from the flats, except for small, controlled amounts allowed through the sluice gates to power the mills. The Cross Dam divided the flats into two receiving basins for this water, which was continuously drained back through the gates into the river. The papers talked a great deal about the marvelous potential afforded by the dam for water-powered mills, mills that would make Boston a giant of commerce and industry.

Charlotte didn't care two cents about commerce and industry. What she cared about was the smell. Mama had been right. The drained tidal basin reeked of rotten fish—and worse. People on the Boston side of the basin dumped their sewage into it. They called it the Back Bay, and it was widely known as a stinking, noxious bowl of filth. The brisk winds that swept across Boston from the Atlantic carried the stench to Roxbury. As the days grew warmer, the smell grew worse.

In June, not long after Ellie's Aunt Ruth married plump Mr. Faxon and moved to his little house on Dudley Street, Charlotte and Lydia returned to Miss Eaton's. On the walk to school, they had to breathe through their mouths all the way to Washington Street. Once they turned toward the main part of town, it wasn't so bad. By the time they reached the common, they could take deep breaths again. Miss Eaton's house was far enough from the flats to be unaffected by the stench.

But on the way home it would assault them again, and Charlotte began to dread the walk down Tide Mill Lane. As spring rolled into summer, the smell grew worse. Mama kept the windows closed despite the heat. The house was stifling as a brick oven, and still the awful odor crept in. Food tasted terrible.

Mama stalked around the kitchen like a furious cat, slamming things down on the worktable. Once she slammed a green tomato and it splattered her in the face. For a moment she looked as though she might burst into flame, she was so angry, and then her sense of humor got the better of her and she laughed.

"That's one way to make a relish," she said, licking tomato seeds off her lip. Charlotte and Mary shrieked with laughter. George scrambled out of Charlotte's lap and scooted across the floor to get his hands on a pulpy wet chunk of tomato. The girls and Mama laughed all the harder.

But the smell was no laughing matter. The garden was suffering, because no one could stand to stay outside in the stench and weed it. Charlotte and Mary didn't play any of their usual summer games in the creek. They stayed in the house with Mama and George, playing at being princesses with long veils draped over their faces. It was hot, but at least the smell was muffled.

One day Papa sat down to dinner, and he shook his head.

"It'll not get any better," he said. "We've got to face facts. This house isna fit to live in any longer. Ye canna walk out the front door wi'out a wagon running ye doon, and ye canna draw a breath wi'out chokin' on it. When a man's wife serves him roast chicken and all he smells is filth, it's time to cut bait. I've been looking at a place in town, and I think we ought to buy it."

The family sat in stunned silence.

"Gah!" said George, looking pleased to have such a quiet audience for his announcement. "Bah gah!"

Charlotte said, "You can't mean it, Papa."

Mama didn't say anything, and Charlotte saw in her eyes that she had known already.

Lydia broke into a smile. "Where is it? The new house?"

Charlotte glared at her. Lydia was actually happy! She wanted to move!

"It can't go on stinking forever," said Charlotte stubbornly. "Or else we'll get used to it. I'm used to it already."

Mama was sympathetic.

"I ken, love," she said softly. "I feel just as you do. If 'twere just the smell . . . but it isn't. The road's so busy. We're livin' on a highway now, and that'll only get worse, even if the smell gets better."

155

Charlotte saw there was no point in talking about it. The others were excited. They wanted to know where the new house was and would Papa sell the smithy, too? No, he said, he wouldn't. He would walk to work from the new place, which was just across the common. A busy road was a good place for a smithy. The very same things that were bad for peaceful living would be good for business.

"What is the house like?" asked Lydia. "Does it have a garden?"

"Aye, o' course it does! And a barn, too. D'ye think I could expect yer mother to live wi'out her herbs and her sheep?"

"We'll dig up the herbs and bring them with us," said Mama. "Tom can tend the vegetable garden here through the summer, and I'll harvest as usual. Next year we can plant at the new place."

The new place. Charlotte hated the way they all talked about it so easily, as if it weren't the most hateful news ever to be announced at that table. It struck her as rude to talk about another house right here in the parlor, where the old house could hear.

She was about to say something cross when she got a look at Mary's face. Her chin was quivering, and she was fighting to hold back tears.

Charlotte reached for her hand under the table and squeezed it, to show she understood. That was too much for Mary, and the tears spilled down her cheeks.

"Och, darlin'," said Mama. "Dinna fret. We're all sad to leave this house. But you'll like the new place, you'll see."

"It won't be the same," said Mary.

"It's not the same *now*," Tom pointed out.

"The devil take that dam," snapped Charlotte.

Papa regarded her beneath lifted brows. She squirmed beneath his gaze.

"You dinna mean that," he said. "Not really. And ye ought not to say what ye dinna mean."

"Yes, Papa," she said meekly.

"It's all right, yer not likin' the dam," he added. "Just make sure ye give the new house a fair chance."

Charlotte nodded. She would not say anything about the new place out loud, for fear of hurting the old house's feelings.

# *Moving Day*

The Mill Dam road, newly named "Western Avenue," opened on the second of July. The city of Boston celebrated with a modest parade along the avenue, consisting of a few wagonloads of officials and a crowd of men on foot. The party trundled across the length of the dam from Beacon Street to Brookline (many with handkerchiefs pressed to their noses).

The Tuckers did not attend the parade; they spent the day loading a wagon with all their household belongings. It was moving day. Mama put Charlotte in charge of George and told her to take him anywhere she liked so long as it was not under her feet.

"Mary, you stay with Lottie," she added. "Keep away from the road, do you hear?"

Charlotte tied a bonnet onto George's head. His hair was coming in thickly now; it was as red as Mama's and Lewis's. He looked like a miniature Lewis, except for the fat cheeks and the lack of side whiskers.

"Let's go visit Lucy," said Charlotte, heaving George onto her hip. He was heavy but pleasant to carry; she loved how his little fists grabbed handfuls of her dress front and back to hold on. He had a way of tilting his head and looking into her face, smiling with his mouth wide open, as if she were the most delightful thing he had ever laid eyes on. In the light of that radiant baby grin, Charlotte felt as if it didn't much matter where she lived, as long as George was there.

She followed Mary out of the house, leaving Mama shouting orders to the boys and

Lydia behind her. Mary raced along the grassy roadside, dangling her bonnet by the strings.

A streak of red flashed in front of Charlotte. She followed it with her eyes to a clump of witch hazel.

"Look, George, a cardinal," she said.

"Buh! Buh!" said George.

Charlotte stopped and stared at him. "Yes, a bird! Did you say bird? Mary, George said 'bird'!"

He was only eight months old, and talking already! Charlotte kissed him all over his fat round face, thunderstruck at his display of genius.

They passed the smithy and came to the crossing of busy Washington Street. Mary was waiting for Charlotte to catch up, but she darted ahead again across the road. Will and Lucy lived just a little way ahead, in the shadow of Great Hill.

Lucy was glad to see them.

"I had an idea some of you Tuckers might

show up here today. How's your mother holding up, Charlotte?"

"She's cross, but only at furniture and crates," said Charlotte, plopping George down on the hooked rug in Lucy's small, tidy parlor. "And at Lewis, because he keeps pretending he's going to drop something and break it."

"Mama says she'll break his head if he does," said Mary, laughing.

Lucy chuckled. "I don't envy her—moving a whole big household like yours. It's lovely to set up housekeeping, though. You'll have fun in the new house."

She spoke lightly but her glance upon Charlotte was cautious. Mama had probably told Lucy that Charlotte wasn't happy about the move.

"Our new room is big," said Mary. "Lydia's going to have a bed all to herself."

They spent the whole morning at Lucy's, playing with William and little Anna, who was a sturdy two-year-old now, and preventing

George from climbing into the cradle on top of tiny baby Josephine.

"Bah, bah!" he crowed, whacking the cradle with enthusiastic fists. It sounded exactly like his word for "bird," but it was obvious to Charlotte that he was now saying "baby" for Josephine.

"You are the cleverest boy," she said, swooping him up in her arms.

Mama had said the family would not stop for a hot dinner today; they would have a light meal of bread, cheese, and cold meat in the kitchen after the bulk of the packing was done. Lucy gave Charlotte a basket to take back with her; it held a mutton pie and some ginger cookies wrapped in a linen napkin.

"Can you manage it, with the baby?" she asked.

"I think so. Mary can carry the basket if it gets too heavy."

"Or the baby," said Mary hopefully.

Lucy chuckled. "That baby's so big, I think he could almost carry you."

# Moving Day

As they passed the quiet, shuttered smithy on the way home, Charlotte's heart began to pound. She knew the house would be stripped bare. It was not her home anymore. The cows and sheep were already gone; Tom and Papa had walked them across the common to the new house early that morning. They would be waiting in the small, weathered barn at the back of the wide lot. The new house was scrubbed and ready. Mama had put up curtains already, to help it feel homier their first night.

Charlotte didn't want it to feel homier. She felt sorry for the old house, stripped of its trimmings even before anyone had said good-bye.

Slowly she approached the dooryard. Mary had run ahead, as usual, and came running back out to say, "Charlotte, come see! It looks so *big* without anything inside!"

Mama was in the lean-to standing on a chair, untying herb bundles from the rafters. Her apron was dirty and locks of hair trailed out from under her white cap.

"There's my wee mannie," she said, climbing off the chair and taking George, who was diving out of Charlotte's arms. "Hungry, I'll warrant. That's fine; I could do wi' a rest. What's in the basket, Lottie?"

"A meat pie and cookies."

Numbly, Charlotte followed Mama into the kitchen. It was empty of furniture and dishes; only a litter of sand, ashes, and bits of crumbled herbs showed what a busy place it had been up till that morning.

All the rooms were like that. Mama put Lucy's mutton pie on the floor in the parlor, and everyone sat around it eating straight from the pie pan. With the bread and cheese and cold sliced beef served on napkins, it was like a picnic. Papa said it put him in mind of the day he and Mama had moved into this house, twenty-one years ago.

"The ink was scarcely dry on our wedding notice," he said, leaning back on his elbows. "We hadn't a stick o' furniture, for I'd been livin' in a boardin'house, and yer mother was just off the boat from Scotland wi' no more than would fit in her trunk. We bought this house from John Heath. Just finished buildin' his new house across yonder field, he had. I was for stayin' on a day or two in the boardin'house until we could buy a bed and a couple o' chairs, but your mother'd have none o' it."

His blue eyes twinkled at Mama. She was smiling eagerly, her eyes alight with happiness. George lay sprawled across her lap, having dozed off after nursing. The red roses on the wallpaper behind her made a crown above her head. A lump was in Charlotte's throat. She could not stand to think of leaving that wallpaper behind. How could Mama bear leaving it, this house she had come to as a bride?

"What did you do?" Lydia asked. "Where did you stay?"

"We made camp right here," said Papa. "In this very room. Your mother made a bed out o'—what was it, petticoats stuffed under a quilt? We used boots for pillows, I believe."

Mama threw a crust of bread at him. "We did no such thing," she retorted. "I had two quilts in my trunk. They made a perfectly fine place to sleep, and we had woolen shawls for pillows. Boots, my eye."

"It sounds lovely, Mama," said Lydia dreamily.

Tom poked Lewis. "Is that what you and Emma will do? Get some old shack and throw blankets on the floor?"

For answer, Lewis pummeled Tom's shoulder until he yelped for mercy.

Mama was indignant.

"Some old shack, indeed. This house is as snug a home as any bride could ever ask. Lewis'll have to work hard to provide such a nest for . . . any lass lucky enough to catch him."

Lewis's ears were as red as his hair. If he had any intention to ask for Emma Dillaway's hand, he wasn't telling. But when he caught Charlotte watching him, he winked at her.

# Moving Day

"I'll warrant Emma Dillaway has a whole chest full of quilts," said Lydia, who never noticed when it was time to change a subject.

Mama came to Lewis's rescue. "We'd best start sweepin' up," she said. "Lottie, can you keep George again? If you sit right here beside me, I think I can shift him over wi'out wakin' him."

Charlotte felt strange, sitting there in the middle of the barren parlor with George sleeping openmouthed in her lap, watching the others swirl around her in a brisk dance of boxes and brooms. Papa and the boys finished loading the wagon; they called Mary to ride with them over to the new house. Lydia and Mama made a last sweep through the rooms, collecting stray buttons and pins, anything useful that had been left behind. Mama hummed as she worked, as if she were doing ordinary chores on an ordinary day. But Charlotte listened to the melodies Mama was humming, and she thought of the words that went with them, and she had an idea that

Mama—though she would never show it—
was sad about leaving, too.

> *Ye banks and braes o' bonny Doon,*
> *How can ye bloom so fresh and fair?*
> *How can ye chant, ye little birds,*
> *And I so weary, full o' care!*
> *Ye'll break my heart, ye little birds,*
> *That wanton thro' the flow'ry thorn!*
> *Ye mind me o' departed joys,*
> *Departed never to return.*

# The New House

The new house was on the corner of Union and Warren Streets, an intersection in the oldest part of Roxbury. It was a large house, wide and square, with ten glass-paned windows gleaming proudly from the front: six windows upstairs, and two downstairs on either side of the vivid green door. For the new house was a painted house. Unlike the Tide Mill Lane place, whose pine boards the years had weathered to a dark, streaky brown, the new house was a spotless, shining white. It had belonged to a successful printer whose wife had a taste for the modern. When Charlotte saw the inside of that house, she understood for the first time what Papa meant when he said business was good. He had made a fair profit on the sale of the stone ledges, too, and would make more when he sold the land and the house on Tide Mill Lane. Already he had had offers from businessmen who saw good prospects in a piece of land so close to the dams.

Business was good, so Papa had been able to afford a very nice house. It had eight rooms: four upstairs and four downstairs. To Charlotte's amazement, almost every single one of them was wallpapered. The kitchen had plain wooden walls, of course, but it was a nice big kitchen with a sizable hearth and a brick oven just like the one in the Tide Mill Lane house. The parlor was papered in a pattern of green vines and white latticework. There was a sitting room with walls of a pretty cream color with large dark-blue flowers in stripes at wide intervals. There was even a dining room, papered in an elegant red floral print. Mama had hung the red curtains from the old parlor in this room, though it was otherwise bare.

"We'll eat in the parlor, same as always, for a while," she explained. "'Twill take us a while to get used to such a fine house as this."

Charlotte felt dazzled by the beauty of the elegant rooms. Lydia was in raptures, exclaiming over every wall and window.

"Lottie, come up to our bedchamber! We can see Miss Eaton's school from here!"

The girls' bedchamber looked out upon Warren Street. At Lydia's urging, Charlotte craned her neck to peer sideways across the roofs of houses down the street. Sure enough, she could see the top of the elm tree that towered over Miss Eaton's house on Warren Street. At least, she could see the top of *an* elm tree, and Lydia swore it was Miss Eaton's.

Their new bedroom was next door to Tom and Lewis's, and across the hall from the room shared by Mama and Papa and George. There was an extra room next to Mama's, for company. It wanted a bed, of course. Lydia's promised new bed had not yet been purchased either. All in good time, Mama said.

Mama seemed to be in every room at once, directing the setting down of each piece of furniture Papa and Lewis carried in from the wagon. Charlotte was given charge of George once again. She slung him on her hip and went outside to look at the yard. There was a scattering of trees around the house: a maple in the dooryard, near the street; a pear studded with tiny ripening fruits on the Warren Street side; a clump of birches near the barn, just like the ones across the road from the old house. The sheep and the cows seemed content in their new quarters. There was a vegetable plot laid out behind the house, and a brown gash of tilled soil where Mama was going to transplant some of her herbs.

On two sides of the house were dirt roads, dusty in the July heat. An oxcart trundled by; many people passed on foot. Some of the men tipped their hats to her as they went by; several of the ladies stopped to admire the baby over the low white fence. Charlotte came around the side of the house and found Mary delightedly picking blossoms from an enormous clump of hollyhocks.

"Look, Charlotte, you can make dolls out of them!" Mary showed her how she was twisting the upturned blossoms in the middle to make waists for tiny magenta ladies with full skirts. Charlotte put George down in the grass and helped Mary improve the dolls by wrapping dandelion stems around the middle for the waists, instead of twisting the blossoms. George hooted with approval at the enchanting texture of grass. He dug his fists in and pulled, rocking himself over onto his back.

"George likes it here," said Mary. "So do I."

Charlotte wasn't ready to go quite that far yet.

Mrs. Waitt stopped by late in the afternoon to deliver a spice cake she had baked for them and to tell them about the Western Avenue parade.

"I passed by your old house on the way home," she said despondently. "Awful lonely it looked, with the windows bare and all. Ah, me, we'll miss you folks as neighbors. It just won't be the same without you."

*It won't be the same, it won't be the same*—the thought was a doleful refrain in Charlotte's head. Nothing would be the same. Lydia was happy for that very reason; she thought it was exciting to make a new start. Charlotte felt little pricklings of excitement over some things—the pear tree, the wallpaper, the thought of living close enough to run over to Ellie Till's whenever she liked. But she didn't want to feel excited, so she squashed the pricklings down.

That night, with beds assembled and the old familiar quilts smoothed over them, chairs and tables arranged to Mama's satisfaction in the new rooms, and the fat round clock ticking like a contented cat on the new sitting-room mantel, Mama sank into her favorite chair and looked around with approving eyes.

"'Tis not home yet," she said, "but it soon will be. Look what a fine view o' the sunset we have in this room. Did ever I tell you," she said suddenly, "of the time your Uncle Duncan and I set out to catch the sun in a wooden pail to bring home to our mother for a present?"

"No!" cried Mary, clapping her hands. She was always excited when Mama started a sentence with "Did ever I tell you." "Tell us now!"

"All right, then," said Mama. "Like this, it was."

And before any of them realized it, they had all drawn near Mama, sitting in chairs or lounging on the soft hooked rug that used to grace the old parlor, wrapped up in her story. Charlotte forgot to be homesick for Tide Mill Lane.

"Teeny wee bairns we were," said Mama. "I could no have been more than four, and Duncan would have been aye six years old. Which meant he was quite grown up, in my opinion, and wise as a king. I dinna ken what put it into our heads that we must have a gift for our mother, but 'twas a matter most urgent and grave in our minds. Duncan was all for givin' her a nice big stone he'd found at the loch. But I insisted she must have something pretty.

"'Like Auld Mary's red shawl,' I said, for that was the loveliest thing in the world, in my opinion.

"'How can we get her a shawl?' Duncan scoffed. 'We havena any money.'

"'We could make one,' I said. He pointed out that we had no wool, and besides, I couldna spin. I couldna knit, either, but that didna occur to me. I remember lookin' around for somethin' to make a shawl out o'. We were outside on the hill that sloped down from my father's house to the loch, sittin' in the heather all rosy-purple wi' bells, and the sun was just touchin' the tops o' the hills behind us. I could see it, glowin' red like a great round ember in the sky.

"'There!' I said, pointin'. Duncan looked, and we agreed 'twas the grandest sight we'd ever seen.

"'Aye, let's get her that,' said Duncan. He was very matter-o'-fact about it, and I didna

178

question him for a second. If my brother said
we could get that sun, we could, and no buts
about it."

Charlotte laughed. She was curled on the
floor with George in her lap pulling at her hair
ribbon. Mary had climbed onto Papa's knees,
her face alight.

"We found a pail in the garden and set off
up the hill. We had to go fast, because we
could see that the sun was sinkin' behind the
hill and we feared it would fall all the way
down to the other side before we could reach
it. Duncan raced ahead o' me, but I climbed
as fast as my wee legs could carry me and I
managed to make it all the way to the top.
Duncan was standin' there starin' sorrowfully
off into the distance, for now we could see
that the great red ball was floating way off in
the sky, far beyond our reach. I started to cry,
but Duncan told me to never mind, we'd get
her somethin' better. We turned around to
head for home—and there was our mother,
walkin' up the hill toward us! She'd seen us
go up from her chamber window, and she

came out to see what mischief we were aye gettin' into. I buried my face in her skirts and sobbed out our tale o' disappointment and heartbreak. She laughed—such a merry, rippling laugh, she had, like a string o' bells jinglin' in the wind—and knelt down to wipe my tears wi' her lace-edged handkerchief that smelled o' rosewater. To this day the smell o' roses brings my mother rushin' into my mind."

Mama paused, looking out the window beyond the sunset. Charlotte cuddled George close, kissing his silky red hair, watching Mama watch the sun. She knew exactly how Mama's mother's laugh must have sounded. It was just like Mama's own laugh.

"Duncan said he was sorry we didna get her the nice present after all. And she said, 'Whatever do you mean? Sure and you did. You brought me up here to look at it, did you not? And if ever a lovelier sight there was in the world, I ken not what it could be.'

"And we stood there, the three o' us, watchin' the sun go down over the hills behind our hill. 'Twas ourselves we gave the present to, Duncan and I, for ever since that day, I've always seen a magic in the settin' o' the sun. All mixed up in my heart it is: the beautiful colors, and my brother's courage, and my mother's hand holdin' mine on the top o' the hill."

# Dust and Ashes

I n August a wave of sickness swept
through Roxbury. One by one the fami-
lies at church were struck with it. Entire
pews were empty. Some people even died.
Mama kept the children home in hopes of
avoiding the illness. But one morning Mary
woke up groaning and shaking, and the next
day Charlotte and Lydia had it too.

Mama was not an herbalist for nothing. She
brewed teas and tonics that brought down the
searing fevers and soothed the tortured stom-
achs. Charlotte felt better after a few miserable

days. By the time she got up, Tom and George were down with it also. She was well enough to sit in the kitchen and hold the baby while Mama tended Tom and Mary.

Mary got better, and Lydia, and Tom. Lewis never got sick at all. But George got worse and worse. Charlotte saw the fear in Mama's eyes and remembered another time she had seen that look. Lewis had been dreadfully ill once with blood poisoning. He had very nearly died.

Charlotte had been only six years old then, but she remembered it vividly. She remembered the ache of fear in her belly. She had been certain Lewis *would* die. But Mama had never given up hope, and Mama had been right. Lewis got better.

So Charlotte was sure George would get better too. She felt sorry for him, gasping his thin, pitiful breaths, his little lips blue. She prayed for God to make him better quickly. It felt good to pray, knowing her prayers would be answered. She felt filled with a comfortable, reassuring faith. She held George on her lap, tilting him upright so he could breathe, smiling encouragement upon him.

Then, one morning, Mama came to the girls and told them in a terrible, broken voice that George had died in the night. She did not couch it in delicate phrases like people used in church: the baby had not "gone to his rest"; he had not "passed over." She put it bluntly, simply. *Our bairn is dead.*

Even so, Charlotte could not take it in. She stared stupidly at Mama, shaking her head.

"No," she said.

Lydia was sobbing. Mary buried her head in Mama's lap and cried out in a high, keening wail. But Charlotte just stared blankly at Mama and said in a flat voice, "No. No, he isn't."

Mama reached out over Mary's head and put a hand on Charlotte's cheek.

"Yes, my love. He's gone. The fever took him early this mornin'."

Charlotte brushed the gentle hand away.

"No, he isn't!" she repeated.

She pushed past Mama and ran out of the room.

Papa met her at the bottom of the stairs and put his strong arms around her, but she shook her head and pulled away. She did not want to be comforted. That would mean there was something to be comforted about. That would make it true.

It could not be true.

Even when Mama brought her, later, to her bedroom where George was lying cold and pale on the red-and-white quilt, Charlotte could not believe it was true. He looked like himself, like George sleeping. He was pale because he was sick. She was pale herself. He was fine. It was not true.

But it was true.

There was a funeral. The Reverend Dr. Porter said words about dust and ashes, words that scattered like dust and ashes into the air. Charlotte stood beside the tiny grave in the churchyard, but she did not cry. Everyone else was weeping. Lydia's whole body shook with sobs, so that Lewis had to hold her up. Someone took Mary away, she was crying so hard. Charlotte did not shed a single tear. She felt like one of the people out of Mama's stories, turned to stone. She went where she was told to go, sat where she was told to sit. When kind-eyed neighbors asked if she wanted anything, a bite to eat, a nice cup of tea, she shrugged and turned away. She did not want to see the sorrow in their eyes.

Uncle Duncan came. He sat beside Mama, holding her hand tightly. Papa squeezed his shoulder and thanked him for coming. Mary climbed into his lap and leaned against his chest. Charlotte watched them but could not feel anything. She did not feel anything at all.

# Mama's Secret

That day was over, and other days came. They were all the same. Neighbors brought meals but did not stay long; they had their own sick to tend. Charlotte ate, worked, slept obediently. She felt Mama's worried eyes upon her, but she shrugged them away.

A week passed, and Charlotte and Lydia were sent back to school. Miss Eaton met them with kind, pitying eyes. Charlotte stared stonily back, refusing to be pitied. She did not join in the musical exercises. At needlework time she took up her sampler and worked quietly while the other girls chattered over their hoops. The needle went up and down, piercing the white linen, spanning the empty space with neat red stitches like tiny bricks.

## Died Aug^st 12^th 1821

In the evenings, when they walked home, Lydia tried to talk to her, but Charlotte did not feel like talking. She felt empty, like a house that everyone had moved out of.

One day Ellie Till was not in school. Miss Eaton said there was illness in her family, someone near death.

Charlotte's head shot up.

"Who?" she cried out. *"Who is dying?"*

She had risen from her seat without realizing it; she stood poised on the balls of her feet, trembling.

Understanding flashed across Miss Eaton's face.

"Oh, my dear," she said hastily, "do not be

distressed. Ellie is safe, and her sisters. It is her great-aunt who is suffering. A very elderly lady, I understand."

Charlotte's fists were clenched before her; she shook her head wildly.

"No! Take it back! It isn't true!"

"Oh, Lottie," gasped Lydia.

"It can't be true," cried Charlotte. "Auntie Rho can't die. I never finished telling her the story."

Miss Eaton looked perplexed; she reached for Charlotte, but Charlotte pushed past her, as she had pushed past Mama on—that other day. Lydia rushed after her, but Charlotte shoved her back with a furious cry.

"Leave me alone!"

Lydia froze, and Charlotte escaped. She ran out of the house, down Warren Street, across the common, past the church. She ran all the way to Tide Mill Lane, a stitch tearing at her side. She did not know where she was going until she was standing in front of the old house.

Its dark, bare windows glared at her accusingly. Charlotte could not stand it looking at her like that. She picked up a rock, hurled it at a window. The glass shattered. The crashing noise shocked Charlotte's ears; she stood frozen, breathing hard.

"It doesn't matter," she said out loud. No one could live there anyway. No one could bear the smell.

The house stared at her with its splintered eye.

"I didn't finish telling her the story," she said. "There was only a little bit left, and I didn't tell it to her."

She had meant to, but spring had come. First she was busy with springtime things, and then she was busy moving, and then she was busy settling in at the new house. One more visit is all it would have taken. Now Auntie Rho was going to die without hearing the end of the story. She would never find out if Ivanhoe married Lady Rowena at long last.

Charlotte knew Auntie Rho would die,

knew it as certainly as she knew her baby brother was gone. She had heard it said time and time again, how sickness fell hardest upon the very old and the very young. In a week's time she would be standing again beside a hole in the ground.

She wanted to run again, but she knew the terrible emptiness would follow her. She thought about going into the house, but she did not want to see where she had played with George. Instead she went slowly through the yard, running her hands along the low stone wall she had played on as a little girl. She saw the barn and thought she would do what Auntie Rho had done during the blizzard: burrow into the hay and stay there.

She went inside, but there was no hay to burrow in, only a few scattered wisps. Torn, straggling spiderwebs trembled in the rank breeze. The smell was horrible. She climbed up into the loft and looked out the window across the festering flats.

She sat there for an hour, two hours, she wasn't sure how long. Then she realized she was half expecting Mama to come after her, just as Mama had found her there once long ago when she was little. But no one came.

It occurred to Charlotte that no one knew where she was. Mama would be worried. The thought pierced at her heart, and she climbed down from the loft.

She was just crossing the threshold when she saw Mama in the dooryard. The relief on Mama's face was so vivid that Charlotte shrank back again.

"Lottie," said Mama, opening her arms. Charlotte moved woodenly toward her but she would not meet her mother's eyes.

"Lottie," Mama repeated, but now there was something very like anger in her voice. "Look at me."

Charlotte would not look. Mama took her by the shoulders. Her hands squeezed hard, so hard it hurt.

"You listen to me," she said fiercely. "This—will—not—break—you!" She gave

Charlotte a little shake in her intensity. "Do you hear me? You *shall not* let it break you! You canna put a wall around your heart, Lottie. If you build a wall against the pain, you keep out the love as well."

She dropped down on her knees in the dust, heedless of her skirt, so that her face was on a level with Charlotte's. Stubbornly Charlotte looked off past Mama's head.

"I canna promise you a life free from pain, Charlotte. You are sufferin' now, and you shall suffer again. 'Tis as certain as breathin'. I have buried four children now—aye, four," she said, catching Charlotte's gasp.

Now at last Charlotte was stunned into meeting her mother's eyes.

"You werena born yet when we lost our first bairn," said Mama. Her voice softened. "She didna live long; only two weeks. Betsy, we called her, the bonny wee thing. Then came Lewis, and when he was but a wee lad, I gave birth to your brother Linus. He came early and was already dead when first I held him in my arms."

She drew a deep breath. Still Charlotte could not speak.

"You were five years old when I lost Nancy. She came early too, and died that same night. You were too young to ken anything about it."

Words came choking out of Charlotte.

"It isn't fair."

Mama smiled, a warm, tender smile full of understanding.

"You heard what Dr. Porter said, Lottie. 'The Lord giveth, and the Lord taketh away.' That's what we always say at a buryin'. I think we fix upon the takin' away and forget that the one we loved was a gift in the first place. A *gift*, Charlotte. Our Georgie was a precious gift, and I'm thankful for every day we had him."

"I want him back," Charlotte whispered. "I don't want him in Heaven. I want him here."

"I know, my love. I know."

The dam burst. Charlotte doubled over with sobs. She wept until her chest ached and her head throbbed. Mama held her, smoothing her hair, wiping her face with her apron. After a while Charlotte realized Mama was crying too.

"I didn't know, Mama," she whispered. "You're always so happy."

"Of course I'm happy, lass. I've a great deal to be happy about."

"That's the same thing Auntie Rho said," Charlotte murmured.

"Did she? When?" asked Mama.

"Last winter. A long time ago."

Charlotte leaned against her mother, feeling her warm strength. She was like a birch tree, slender and pliant and strong. She smelled like George. Maybe it was that George had smelled like Mama.

Nancy, Linus, Betsy, her never-known brother and sisters. She had not known to include them on her family record sampler. Their names thrummed in her heart like the notes of the church organ. George was not just a note; he was a whole song. She missed him so much, she could hardly breathe. She thought it would always be with her, that terrible ache in her heart. But the ache was better than the *nothing* had been.

It crossed Charlotte's mind that she had been right about Mama after all. Mama *had* carried a sorrowful secret beneath her merry smile. But it was not at all the kind of secret Charlotte had imagined. Mama was even braver than Charlotte had guessed. But she was not bitter, not even now, when the merry light had been quenched by grief.

And suddenly Charlotte had a flash of understanding. That light had been quenched before, three times at least, and it had always come back. She thought of what her life would have been like without that light, without the laughter in Mama's eyes, and she shuddered. She clung to her mother, feeling a wave of love, salty and strong as the tide, rushing over her, filling her up.

"Come," said Mama, rising to her feet, bringing Charlotte up with her. "Let's go home."

# The End of the Story

O
n a clear day early in September Papa
took the family to walk on the new
dam road to Boston. It was Saturday,
Charlotte and Lydia's half day at school.

"We're about the last folks in town to try it
out," Papa said at breakfast. "We'll go after
the noon meal."

Ellie Till was not at Miss Eaton's again that
day. She had missed many days since the day
Charlotte first learned Auntie Rho was ill.
Mrs. Till needed her at home to help nurse
the dying old woman.

Every day when Charlotte came home from school, she had a lump of dread in her stomach, waiting to hear the news she knew must come before long. Mama always told her first thing whether there had been any word that day. The report was always the same: no change, still very ill, time will tell.

Today when Charlotte came into the kitchen, Mama shook her head and said, "I've not heard yet. I just sent Tom over with a new bottle o' cough tincture. I expect him back any minute."

Charlotte was supposed to set the table for dinner, but mostly she stood gripping the plates, biting her lip, lost in thought, waiting for Tom to come back with the news she did not want to hear.

All too soon he burst into the kitchen, snatching up a doughnut from the jar on the sideboard and eating half of it in one gulp. Mama looked up from her dishpan. Charlotte felt Lydia looking at her.

"How is she?" Mama asked. Charlotte stood

rooted to the floor, rigid as the broom handle.

Tom's words were muffled with doughnut. Charlotte heard "gone." She heard "peace." She nodded. She had known it would be so. Auntie Rho was gone. She was at peace.

"Oh, thank the Lord," said Mama, clasping her wet hands. Lydia was smiling, wiping her eyes. Charlotte stared at them stupidly, wondering if there was something mean and selfish about her soul that she could not rejoice that Auntie Rho's suffering was over.

"Isn't it wonderful, Lottie?" cried Lydia. "It's a miracle."

Charlotte looked at each of them in turn: Lydia, Mama, Tom. They were all beaming at her. It felt strange as a dream; it did not make sense.

"Tom," she said, "tell me again what you said."

He swallowed down the last of his doughnut.

"Her fever is gone and she's resting peacefully," he said, speaking slowly and carefully as if to a tiny child. "They think she's going to be all right."

"She's going to be all right," Charlotte echoed, still not grasping it.

"That's what Ellie's mother thinks," said Tom. "They all think so."

"She's going to be all right," said Charlotte again. Mama laughed.

"That's it, my love," she said. "Keep tellin' yourself until you believe it!"

Papa and Lewis came home from the smithy, and the family ate a hurried meal. After a hasty washing of dishes, they set off walking across the common, past the church, along Washington Street, past Waitt's mill, past Papa's blacksmith shop. They continued down Tide Mill Lane, where tall purple asters grew thickly along the roadsides.

Everyone looked at the old house, dark and empty, as they passed. Charlotte's cheeks burned at the sight of the broken window. She was afraid someone would say something, but Mama began to talk with great animation about the improvements they needed to make to the new barn before winter set in, and the house was far behind them before Tom and Lewis finished declaring their plans for the new hayloft.

The drained flats gave off their rank, fishy smell, but the cool September air had mellowed it a little. They came to the Cross Dam. Tom raced Mary to see who would be first to set foot on the new road that reached its gray puddingstone arm across the water. He let her win, of course. But then Lewis thundered up behind her and leapfrogged right over Mary's startled head, causing Mama to shriek and Mary to nearly fall over. Lewis guffawed.

"Do it again," cried Mary, causing Mama to howl with laughter.

"Hush," said Lydia, as if she were the mother. "What will people think?"

"There's no one about to think anything at all," said Mama, for they were the only ones on the road just then, except for a wagon far ahead of them on the dam road, headed, as they were, toward Boston.

Boston loomed before them so astonishingly close, closer with each step, that Charlotte felt a tiny, reluctant softening of her heart toward the hated Mill Dam. All her life she had wanted to go to Boston. And now she was going. There it was, just down the road. They came to the point where the Cross Dam met the big Mill Dam. Turning east, they walked between the slim young trees planted on either side of the Mill Dam road. Western Avenue, Charlotte corrected herself. This was the new Western Avenue that stretched all the way across the Charles River from the Boston town common to the village of Brookline, far behind them on the other side.

"I see the State House," said Lydia. She pointed to the glitter of a domed roof in the distance. That was the famous copper dome that Paul Revere and his brother had worked on so many years before Charlotte was born.

"There's Beacon Hill," said Lewis, nodding at the green mound off to their left.

They left the dam road and found themselves on Beacon Street, at the edge of the common. It looked much like the Roxbury town common, only bigger. Cows and sheep grazed on the thick grass, and small boys rolled wagon hoops between them. Beacon Street was crowded now, noisy, full of women with big straw baskets and men with sacks slung over their backs. There was a bustling let's-get-home-to-supper urgency in the air. Charlotte felt as if she were waking up after a dream. She looked around eagerly, wanting to see everything at once. Boston. She was really in Boston at last.

They came to a row of shops, and Mama said she'd like to look at some printed cotton. Papa and the boys ducked into a hat shop next door to the dry goods store in whose window Mama had spotted some enticing bolts of cloth. The girls followed her in eagerly. The store's shelves were packed with a dizzying array of merchandise, from kitchen utensils to cones of sugar to tins of tobacco. Mama went straight to the huge bank of shelves lined with neat rolls of fabric, in every color Charlotte had ever seen or heard of.

"Ooh, look at the ribbons," Mary cried, tugging on Charlotte's arm. They leaned over a glass case filled with spools of beautiful satin ribbon, wide and thin, with labels proclaiming their various merits in delicate script.

## China Silk, Imported
### Finest Ladies' Satin Trim

"Ten yards of the blue, if you please," Mama said to the merchant, pointing at a pretty chintz on a high shelf. "Girls, what do you think?"

"Mama," said Charlotte, struck with a sudden thought, "might I buy a bit of hair ribbon? Just a small piece?"

Mama looked amused. "Not too small, surely? You've rather a thick mane, my lass."

Charlotte shook her head. "Not for me. For Auntie Rho. She likes something pretty to tie her braid."

Mama touched Charlotte's cheek. "Of course you may, Lottie."

"Ooh, what color, Charlotte?" cried Mary. "How about this scarlet? It's awfully nice."

"No, she has a red ribbon." Charlotte scanned the rainbow of spools, searching. "There. The sea-green one. Just like Lady Rowena's gown."

She couldn't wait to go and see Auntie Rho, to curl up in her spot on the foot of the big curtained bed and tell her the last chapter of *Ivanhoe*. Already she could see the eager light in Auntie Rho's eyes, leaning back on her throne of pillows with the girlish braid slung saucily over her shoulder.

"Now *that's* what I call a story," she would say. And she would be right, as usual.

The afternoon slipped quickly away: a cheese shop, a stationer's shop, a stop into a bakery for some buns to eat as they walked, and Mama said it was time to go home. Mary begged to stay just a little longer, until the gaslights came on, but Papa said they'd best get home to the livestock and supper.

"'Twill be a late one, as it is," he said, pointing to the western sky. They were back on Beacon Street, nearing the river and the dam. The sun hung huge and golden above the far shore, casting nets of pink and orange and copper cloud into the deepening blue sky. Already a speck of star glimmered in one rosy net, like a tiny silver fish. It was so lovely it took Charlotte's breath away. She saw how Mama's eyes smiled at the sunset, and she knew Mama was seeing more than cloud and sun and sky. She was seeing her own mother, and Uncle Duncan, and all the family she had left so far behind to follow Papa across the ocean. Charlotte could see them too. She thought of George, imagined him shining like a star in that blue-and-gold sea, and the other babies twinkling beside him.

She stood there for a long moment with

Mama and Papa and her sisters and brothers, hushed, faces lifted toward the sun. Then they struck out together for home along the new dam road.